MERMAID TALES

THE LITTLE MERMAID AND 14 OTHER ILLUSTRATED MERMAID STORIES

Fairytalez

MERMAID TALES
The Little Mermaid and 14 Other Illustrated Mermaid Stories

Published by Fairytalez.com
www.fairytalez.com

©2016 Fairytalez™

Edited by Bri Ahearn
Cover design and interior art by Loreta Petkova
Cover illustration by Jennie Harbour

Contents

Foreword

Who would be a mermaid fair,
Singing alone, Combing her hair
Under the sea, In a golden curl
With a comb of pearl, On a throne?

ALFRED LORD TENNYSON

A legend that has captivated the world for centuries is that of the mermaid. She is a creature of the water, and it's the sea that gives the mermaid her name: mer is from the Old English word mere which means sea. Known for her beauty, the mermaid is a mystical creature who is frequently portrayed as half-woman, half-fish.

The mermaid's mythology dates back as far as 1000 B.C., and the creature has a presence in cultures throughout the world. In France, the mermaid is often seen as a serpent-woman, sometimes depicted with two tailes, known as Melusine. Scottish folklore is imbued with belief in selkies (silkie), beautiful women who cloak themselves in seal skin to swim in the water. The Celts believed in a mermaid figure known as the merrow, while in China, mermaids are considered water spirits.

"Bronze mermaid from the Middle East dating back 3000 years"

As figures that have stirred the imagination of poets, artists, and authors for years, mermaids are timeless figures of beauty, intrigue, and desire. Here you'll find the familiar Hans Christian Andersen tale The Little Mermaid, but also less-familiar stories from Poland, Spain, Estonia, China and North America. Each tale has been handed down in the culture through generations - some are long forgotten, while others are still just as present in the culture today. If you want to dive more into the folklore of not just the mermaid, but a number of wondrous creatures and people, please visit: Fairytalez.com.

Bri Ahearn, Fairytalez.com

Denmark

The Little Mermaid

Hans Christian Andersen

Illustrations David Burliuk (cover) and Helen Stratton

Editor's Note: *You may find this story has a surprising ending, and is much different compared to the Disney animated movie. It is, however, a beloved fairy tale from a master.*

F ar out in the ocean, where the water is as blue as the prettiest cornflower and as clear as crystal, it is very, very deep; so deep, indeed, that no cable could sound it, and many church steeples, piled one upon another, would not reach from the ground beneath to the surface of the water above. There dwell the Sea King and his subjects. We must not imagine that there is nothing at the bottom of the sea but bare yellow sand. No, indeed, for on this sand grow the strangest flowers and plants, the leaves and stems of which are so pliant that the slightest agitation of the water causes them to stir as if they had life. Fishes, both large and small, glide between the branches as birds fly among the trees here upon land.

In the deepest spot of all stands the castle of the Sea King. Its walls are built of coral, and the long Gothic windows are of the clearest amber. The roof is formed of shells that open and close as the water flows over them. Their appearance is very beautiful, for in each lies a glittering pearl which would be fit for the diadem of a queen.

The Sea King had been a widower for many years, and his aged mother kept house for him. She was a very sensible woman, but exceedingly proud of her high birth, and on that account wore twelve oysters on her tail, while others of high rank were only allowed to wear six.

She was, however, deserving of very great praise, especially for her care of the little sea princesses, her six granddaughters. They were beautiful children, but the youngest was the prettiest of them all. Her skin was as clear and delicate as a rose leaf, and her eyes as blue as the deepest sea; but, like all the others, she had no feet and her body ended in a fish's tail. All day long they played in the great halls of the castle or among the living flowers that grew out of the walls. The large amber windows were open, and the fish swam in, just as the swallows fly into our houses when we open the windows; only the fishes swam up to the princesses, ate out of their hands, and allowed themselves to be stroked.

"Ate out of their hands, and allowed themselves to be stroked."

Outside the castle there was a beautiful garden, in which grew bright-red and dark-blue flowers, and blossoms like flames of fire; the fruit glittered like gold, and the leaves and stems waved to and fro continually. The earth itself was the finest sand, but blue as the flame of burning sulphur. Over everything lay a peculiar blue radiance, as if the blue sky were everywhere, above and below, instead of the dark depths of the sea. In calm weather the sun could be seen, looking like a reddish-purple flower with light streaming from the calyx.

Each of the young princesses had a little plot of ground in the garden, where she might dig and plant as she pleased. One arranged her flower bed in the form of a whale; another preferred to make hers like the figure of a little mermaid; while the youngest child made hers round, like the sun, and in it grew flowers as red as his rays at sunset.

She was a strange child, quiet and thoughtful. While her sisters showed delight at the wonderful things which they obtained from the wrecks of vessels, she cared only for her pretty flowers, red like the sun, and a beautiful marble statue. It was the representation of a handsome boy, carved out of pure white stone, which had fallen to the bottom of the sea from a wreck.

She planted by the statue a rose-colored weeping willow. It grew rapidly and soon hung its fresh branches over the statue, almost down to the blue sands. The shadows had the color of violet and waved to and fro like the branches, so that it seemed as if the crown of the tree and the root were at play, trying to kiss each other.

Nothing gave her so much pleasure as to hear about the world above the sea. She made her old grandmother tell her all she knew of the ships and of the towns, the people and the animals. To her it seemed most wonderful and beautiful to hear that the flowers of the land had fragrance, while those below the sea had none; that the trees of the forest were green; and that the fishes among the trees could sing so sweetly that it was a pleasure to listen to them. Her grandmother called the birds fishes, or the little mermaid would not have understood what was meant, for she had never seen birds.

"When you have reached your fifteenth year," said the grandmother," you will have permission to rise up out of the sea and sit on the rocks in the moonlight, while the great ships go sailing by. Then you will see both forests and towns."

In the following year, one of the sisters would be fifteen, but as each was a year younger than the other, the youngest would have to wait five years before her turn came to rise up from the bottom of the ocean to see the earth as we do. However, each promised to tell the others what she saw on her first visit and what she thought was most beautiful. Their grandmother could not tell them enough—there were so many things about which they wanted to know.

None of them longed so much for her turn to come as the youngest—she who had the longest time to wait and who was so quiet and thoughtful. Many nights she stood by the open window, looking up through the dark blue water and watching the fish as they splashed about with their fins and tails. She could see the moon and stars shining faintly, but through the water they looked larger than they do to our eyes. When something like a black cloud passed between her and them, she knew that it was either a whale swimming over her head, or a ship full of human beings who never imagined that a pretty little mermaid was standing beneath them, holding out her white hands towards the keel of their ship.

At length the eldest was fifteen and was allowed to rise to the surface of the ocean. When she returned she had hundreds of things to talk about. But the finest thing, she said, was to lie on a sand bank in the quiet moonlit sea, near the shore, gazing at the lights of the near-by town, that twinkled like hundreds of stars, and listening to the sounds of music, the noise of carriages, the voices of human beings, and the merry pealing of the bells in the church steeples. Because she could not go near all these wonderful things, she longed for them all the more.

Oh, how eagerly did the youngest sister listen to all these descriptions! And afterwards, when she stood at the open window looking up through the dark-blue water, she thought of the great city, with all its bustle and noise, and even fancied she could hear the sound of the church bells down in the depths of the sea.

In another year the second sister received permission to rise to the surface of the water and to swim about where she pleased. She rose just as the sun was setting, and this, she said, was the most beautiful sight of all. The whole sky looked like gold, and violet and rose-colored clouds, which she could not describe, drifted across it. And more swiftly than the clouds, flew a large flock of wild swans toward the setting sun, like a long white veil across the sea. She also swam towards the sun, but it sank into the waves, and the rosy tints faded from the clouds and from the sea.

The third sister's turn followed, and she was the boldest of them all, for she swam up a broad river that emptied into the sea. On the banks she saw green hills covered with beautiful vines, and palaces and castles peeping out from amid the proud trees of the forest. She heard birds singing and felt the rays of the sun so strongly that she was obliged often to dive under the water to cool her burning face. In a narrow creek she found a large group of little human children, almost naked, sporting about in the water. She wanted to play with them, but they fled in a great fright; and then a little black animal—it was a dog, but she did not know it, for she had never seen one before—came to the water and barked at her so furiously that she became frightened and rushed back to the open sea. But she said she should never forget the beautiful forest, the green hills, and the pretty children who could swim in the water although they had no tails.

"They fled in a great fright."

The fourth sister was more timid. She remained in the midst of the sea, but said it was quite as beautiful there as nearer the land. She could see many miles around her, and the sky above looked like a bell of glass. She had seen the ships, but at such a great distance that they looked like sea gulls. The dolphins sported in the waves, and the great whales spouted water from their nostrils till it seemed as if a hundred fountains were playing in every direction.

The fifth sister's birthday occurred in the winter, so when her turn came she saw what the others had not seen the first time they went up. The sea looked quite green, and large icebergs were floating about, each like a pearl, she said, but larger and loftier than the churches built by men. They were of the most singular shapes and glittered like diamonds. She had seated herself on one of the largest and let the wind play with her long hair. She noticed that all the ships sailed past very rapidly, steering as far away as they could, as if they were afraid of the iceberg. Towards evening, as the sun went down, dark clouds covered the sky, the thunder rolled, and the flashes of lightning glowed red on the icebergs as they were tossed about by the heaving sea. On all the ships the sails were reefed with fear and trembling, while she sat on the floating iceberg, calmly watching the lightning as it darted its forked flashes into the sea.

Each of the sisters, when first she had permission to rise to the surface, was delighted with the new and beautiful sights. Now that they were grown-up girls and could go when they pleased, they had become quite indifferent about it. They soon wished themselves back again, and after a month had passed they said it was much more beautiful down below and pleasanter to be at home.

Yet often, in the evening hours, the five sisters would twine their arms about each other and rise to the surface together. Their voices were more charming than that of any human being, and before the approach of a storm, when they feared that a ship might be lost, they swam before the vessel, singing enchanting songs of the delights to be found in the depths of the sea and begging the voyagers not to fear if they sank to the bottom. But the sailors could not understand the song and thought it was the sighing of the storm. These things were never beautiful to them, for if the ship sank, the men were drowned and their dead bodies alone reached the palace of the Sea King. When the sisters rose, arm in arm, through the water, their youngest sister would stand quite alone, looking after them, ready to cry—only, since mermaids have no tears, she suffered more acutely.

"Oh, were I but fifteen years old!" said she. "I know that I shall love the world up there, and all the people who live in it."

"All the vessels scudded past in great alarm."

At last she reached her fifteenth year.

"Well, now you are grown up," said the old dowager, her grandmother. "Come, and let me adorn you like your sisters." And she placed in her hair a wreath of white lilies, of which every flower leaf was half a pearl. Then the old lady ordered eight great oysters to attach themselves to the tail of the princess to show her high rank.

"But they hurt me so," said the little mermaid.

"Yes, I know; pride must suffer pain," replied the old lady.

Oh, how gladly she would have shaken off all this grandeur and laid aside the heavy wreath! The red flowers in her own garden would have suited her much better. But she could not change herself, so she said farewell and rose as lightly as a bubble to the surface of the water.

The sun had just set when she raised her head above the waves. The clouds were tinted with crimson and gold, and through the glimmering twilight beamed the evening star in all its beauty. The sea was calm, and the air mild and fresh. A large ship with three masts lay becalmed on the water; only one sail was set, for not a breeze stirred, and the sailors sat idle on deck or amidst the rigging. There was music and song on board, and as darkness came on, a hundred colored lanterns were lighted, as if the flags of all nations waved in the air.

The little mermaid swam close to the cabin windows, and now and then, as the waves lifted her up, she could look in through glass window-panes and see a number of gayly dressed people. Among them, and the most beautiful of all, was a young prince with large, black eyes. He was sixteen years of age, and his birthday was being celebrated with great display. The sailors were dancing on deck, and when the prince came out of the cabin, more than a hundred rockets rose in the air, making it as bright as day. The little mermaid was so startled that she dived under water, and when she again stretched out her head, it looked as if all the stars of heaven were falling around her.

She had never seen such fireworks before. Great suns spurted fire about, splendid fireflies flew into the blue air, and everything was reflected in the clear, calm sea beneath. The ship itself was so brightly illuminated that all the people, and even the smallest rope, could be distinctly seen. How handsome the young prince looked, as he pressed the hands of all his guests and smiled at them, while the music resounded through the clear night air!

It was very late, yet the little mermaid could not take her eyes from the ship or from the beautiful prince. The colored lanterns had been extinguished, no more rockets rose in the air, and the cannon had ceased firing; but the sea became restless, and a moaning, grumbling sound could be heard beneath the waves.

Still the little mermaid remained by the cabin window, rocking up and down on the water, so that she could look within.

After a while the sails were quickly set, and the ship went on her way. But soon the waves rose higher, heavy clouds darkened the sky, and lightning appeared in the distance. A dreadful storm was approaching. Once more the sails were furled, and the great ship pursued her flying course over the raging sea. The waves rose mountain high, as if they would overtop the mast, but the ship dived like a swan between them, then rose again on their lofty, foaming crests. To the little mermaid this was pleasant sport; but not so to the sailors. At length the ship groaned and creaked; the thick planks gave way under the lashing of the sea, as the waves broke over the deck; the mainmast snapped asunder like a reed, and as the ship lay over on her side, the water rushed in.

The little mermaid now perceived that the crew were in danger; even she was obliged to be careful, to avoid the beams and planks of the wreck which lay scattered on the water. At one moment it was pitch dark so that she could not see a single object, but when a flash of lightning came it revealed the whole scene; she could see everyone who had been on board except the prince. When the ship parted, she had seen him sink into the deep waves, and she was glad, for she thought he would now be with her. Then she remembered that human beings could not live in the water, so that when he got down to her father's palace he would certainly be quite dead.

No, he must not die! So she swam about among the beams and planks which strewed the surface of the sea, forgetting that they could crush her to pieces. Diving deep under the dark waters, rising and falling with the waves, she at length managed to reach the young prince, who was fast losing the power to swim in that stormy sea. His limbs were failing him, his beautiful eyes were closed, and he would have died had not the little mermaid come to his assistance. She held his head above the water and let the waves carry them where they would.

"She had his head above the water and let the waves carry them where they would."

In the morning the storm had ceased, but of the ship not a single fragment could be seen. The sun came up red and shining out of the water, and its beams brought back the hue of health to the prince's cheeks, but his eyes remained closed. The mermaid kissed his high, smooth forehead and stroked back his wet hair. He seemed to her like the marble statue in her little garden, so she kissed him again and wished that he might live.

Presently they came in sight of land, and she saw lofty blue mountains on which the white snow rested as if a flock of swans were lying upon them. Beautiful green forests were near the shore, and close by stood a large building, whether a church or a convent she could not tell. Orange and citron trees grew in the garden, and before the door stood lofty palms. The sea here formed a little bay, in which the water lay quiet and still, but very deep. She swam with the handsome prince to the beach, which was covered with fine white sand, and there she laid him in the warm sunshine, taking care to raise his head higher than his body. Then bells sounded in the large white building, and some young girls came into the garden. The little mermaid swam out farther from the shore and hid herself among some high rocks that rose out of the water. Covering her head and neck with the foam of the sea, she watched there to see what would become of the poor prince.

It was not long before she saw a young girl approach the spot where the prince lay. She seemed frightened at first, but only for a moment; then she brought a number of people, and the mermaid saw that the prince came to life again and smiled upon those who stood about him. But to her he sent no smile; he knew not that she had saved him. This made her very sorrowful, and when he was led away into the great building, she dived down into the water and returned to her father's castle.

"It was not long before she saw a young girl approach the spot where the prince lay."

She had always been silent and thoughtful, and now she was more so than ever. Her sisters asked her what she had seen during her first visit to the surface of the water, but she could tell them nothing. Many an evening and morning did she rise to the place where she had left the prince. She saw the fruits in the garden ripen and watched them gathered; she watched the snow on the mountain tops melt away; but never did she see the prince, and therefore she always returned home more sorrowful than before.

It was her only comfort to sit in her own little garden and fling her arm around the beautiful marble statue, which was like the prince. She gave up tending her flowers, and they grew in wild confusion over the paths, twining their long leaves and stems round the branches of the trees so that the whole place became dark and gloomy. At length she could bear it no longer and told one of her sisters all about it. Then the others heard the secret, and very soon it became known to several mermaids, one of whom had an intimate friend who happened to know about the prince. She had also seen the festival on board ship, and she told them where the prince came from and where his palace stood.

"Come, little sister," said the other princesses. Then they entwined their arms and rose together to the surface of the water, near the spot where they knew the prince's palace stood. It was built of bright-yellow, shining stone and had long flights of marble steps, one of which reached quite down to the sea. Splendid gilded cupolas rose over the roof, and between the pillars that surrounded the whole building stood lifelike statues of marble. Through the clear crystal of the lofty windows could be seen noble rooms, with costly silk curtains and hangings of tapestry and walls covered with beautiful paintings. In the center of the largest salon a fountain threw its sparkling jets high up into the glass cupola of the ceiling, through which the sun shone in upon the water and upon the beautiful plants that grew in the basin of the fountain.

Now that the little mermaid knew where the prince lived, she spent many an evening and many a night on the water near the palace. She would swim much nearer the shore than any of the others had ventured, and once she went up the narrow channel under the marble balcony, which threw a broad shadow on the water. Here she sat and watched the young prince, who thought himself alone in the bright moonlight.

She often saw him evenings, sailing in a beautiful boat on which music sounded and flags waved. She peeped out from among the green rushes, and if the wind caught her long silvery-white veil, those who saw it believed it to be a swan, spreading out its wings.

Many a night, too, when the fishermen set their nets by the light of their torches, she heard them relate many good things about the young prince. And this made her glad that she had saved his life when he was tossed about half dead on the waves. She remembered how his head had rested on her bosom and how heartily she had kissed him, but he knew nothing of all this and could not even dream of her.

She grew more and more to like human beings and wished more and more to be able to wander about with those whose world seemed to be so much larger than her own. They could fly over the sea in ships and mount the high hills which were far above the clouds; and the lands they possessed, their woods and their fields, stretched far away beyond the reach of her sight. There was so much that she wished to know! but her sisters were unable to answer all her questions. She then went to her old grandmother, who knew all about the upper world, which she rightly called "the lands above the sea."

"If human beings are not drowned," asked the little mermaid, "can they live forever? Do they never die, as we do here in the sea?"

"Yes," replied the old lady, "they must also die, and their term of life is even shorter than ours. We sometimes live for three hundred years, but when we cease to exist here, we become only foam on the surface of the water and have not even a grave among those we love. We have not immortal souls, we shall never live again; like the green seaweed when once it has been cut off, we can never flourish more. Human beings, on the contrary, have souls which live forever, even after the body has been turned to dust. They rise up through the clear, pure air, beyond the glittering stars. As we rise out of the water and behold all the land of the earth, so do they rise to unknown and glorious regions which we shall never see."

"Why have not we immortal souls?" asked the little mermaid, mournfully. "I would gladly give all the hundreds of years that I have to live, to be a human being only for one day and to have the hope of knowing the happiness of that glorious world above the stars."

"You must not think that," said the old woman. "We believe that we are much happier and much better off than human beings."

"'You must not think that', said the old woman."

"So I shall die," said the little mermaid, "and as the foam of the sea I shall be driven about, never again to hear the music of the waves or to see the pretty flowers or the red sun? Is there anything I can do to win an immortal soul?"

"No," said the old woman; "unless a man should love you so much that you were more to him than his father or his mother, and if all his thoughts and all his love were fixed upon you, and the priest placed his right hand in yours, and he promised to be true to you here and hereafter—then his soul would glide into your body, and you would obtain a share in the future happiness of mankind. He would give to you a soul and retain his own as well; but this can never happen. Your fish's tail, which among us is considered so beautiful, on earth is thought to be quite ugly. They do not know any better, and they think it necessary, in order to be handsome, to have two stout props, which they call legs."

Then the little mermaid sighed and looked sorrowfully at her fish's tail. "Let us be happy," said the old lady, "and dart and spring about during the three hundred years that we have to live, which is really quite long enough. After that we can rest ourselves all the better. This evening we are going to have a court ball."

It was one of those splendid sights which we can never see on earth. The walls and the ceiling of the large ballroom were of thick but transparent crystal. Many hundreds of colossal shells,—some of a deep red, others of a grass green,—with blue fire in them, stood in rows on each side. These lighted up the whole salon, and shone through the walls so that the sea was also illuminated. Innumerable fishes, great and small, swam past the crystal walls; on some of them the scales glowed with a purple brilliance, and on others shone like silver and gold. Through the halls flowed a broad stream, and in it danced the mermen and the mermaids to the music of their own sweet singing.

No one on earth has such lovely voices as they, but the little mermaid sang more sweetly than all. The whole court applauded her with hands and tails, and for a moment her heart felt quite gay, for she knew she had the sweetest voice either on earth or in the sea. But soon she thought again of the world above her; she could not forget the charming prince, nor her sorrow that she had not an immortal soul like his. She crept away silently out of her father's palace, and while everything within was gladness and song, she sat in her own little garden, sorrowful and alone. Then she heard the bugle sounding through the water and thought: "He is certainly sailing above, he in whom my wishes center and in whose hands I should like to place the happiness of my life. I will venture all for him and to win an immortal soul. While my sisters are dancing in my father's palace I will go to the sea witch, of whom I have always been so much afraid; she can give me counsel and help."

Then the little mermaid went out from her garden and took the road to the foaming whirlpools, behind which the sorceress lived. She had never been that way before. Neither flowers nor grass grew there; nothing but bare, gray, sandy ground stretched out to the whirlpool, where the water, like foaming mill wheels, seized everything that came within its reach and cast it into the fathomless deep. Through the midst of these crushing whirlpools the little mermaid was obliged to pass before she could reach the dominions of the sea witch. Then, for a long distance, the road lay across a stretch of warm, bubbling mire, called by the witch her turf moor.

Beyond this was the witch's house, which stood in the center of a strange forest, where all the trees and flowers were polypi, half animals and half plants. They looked like serpents with a hundred heads, growing out of the ground. The branches were long, slimy arms, with fingers like flexible worms, moving limb after limb from the root to the top. All that could be reached in the sea they seized upon and held fast, so that it never escaped from their clutches.

The little mermaid was so alarmed at what she saw that she stood still and her heart beat with fear. She came very near turning back, but she thought of the prince and of the human soul for which she longed, and her courage returned. She fastened her long, flowing hair round her head, so that the polypi should not lay hold of it. She crossed her hands on her bosom, and then darted forward as a fish shoots through the water, between the supple arms and fingers of the ugly polypi, which were stretched out on each side of her. She saw that they all held in their grasp something they had seized with their numerous little arms, which were as strong as iron bands. Tightly grasped in their clinging arms were white skeletons of human beings who had perished at sea and had sunk down into the deep waters; skeletons of land animals; and oars, rudders, and chests, of ships. There was even a little mermaid whom they had caught and strangled, and this seemed the most shocking of all to the little princess.

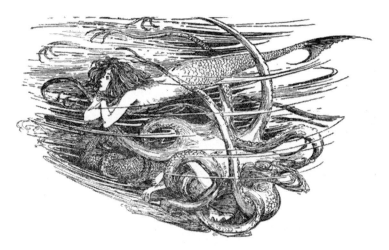

"She crossed her hands on her bosom, and then darted forward as a fish shoots through the water, between the supple arms and fingers of the ugly polypi."

She now came to a space of marshy ground in the wood, where large, fat water snakes were rolling in the mire and showing their ugly, drab-colored bodies. In the midst of this spot stood a house, built of the bones of shipwrecked human beings. There sat the sea witch, allowing a toad to eat from her mouth just as people sometimes feed a canary with pieces of sugar. She called the ugly water snakes her little chickens and allowed them to crawl all over her bosom.

"I know what you want," said the sea witch. "It is very stupid of you, but you shall have your way, though it will bring you to sorrow, my pretty princess. You want to get rid of your fish's tail and to have two supports instead, like human beings on earth, so that the young prince may fall in love with you and so that you may have an immortal soul." And then the witch laughed so loud and so disgustingly that the toad and the snakes fell to the ground and lay there wriggling.

"You are but just in time," said the witch, "for after sunrise tomorrow I should not be able to help you till the end of another year. I will prepare a draft for you, with which you must swim to land tomorrow before sunrise; seat yourself there and drink it. Your tail will then disappear, and shrink up into what men call legs."

"You will feel great pain, as if a sword were passing through you. But all who see you will say that you are the prettiest little human being they ever saw. You will still have the same floating gracefulness of movement, and no dancer will ever tread so lightly. Every step you take, however, will be as if you were treading upon sharp knives and as if the blood must flow. If you will bear all this, I will help you."

"Yes, I will," said the little princess in a trembling voice, as she thought of the prince and the immortal soul.

"But think again," said the witch, "for when once your shape has become like a human being, you can no more be a mermaid. You will never return through the water to your sisters or to your father's palace again. And if you do not win the love of the prince, so that he is willing to forget his father and mother for your sake and to love you with his whole soul and allow the priest to join your hands that you may be man and wife, then you will never have an immortal soul. The first morning after he marries another, your heart will break and you will become foam on the crest of the waves."

"I will do it," said the little mermaid, and she became pale as death.

"But I must be paid, also," said the witch, "and it is not a trifle that I ask. You have the sweetest voice of any who dwell here in the depths of the sea, and you believe that you will be able to charm the prince with it. But this voice you must give to me. The best thing you possess will I have as the price of my costly draft, which must be mixed with my own blood so that it may be as sharp as a two-edged sword."

"But if you take away my voice," said the little mermaid, "what is left for me?"

"Your beautiful form, your graceful walk, and your expressive eyes. Surely with these you can enchain a man's heart. Well, have you lost your courage? Put out your little tongue, that I may cut it off as my payment; then you shall have the powerful draft."

"It shall be," said the little mermaid.

Then the witch placed her caldron on the fire, to prepare the magic draft.

"Cleanliness is a good thing," said she, scouring the vessel with snakes which she had tied together in a large knot. Then she pricked herself in the breast and let the black blood drop into the caldron. The steam that rose twisted itself into such horrible shapes that no one could look at them without fear. Every moment the witch threw a new ingredient into the vessel, and when it began to boil, the sound was like the weeping of a crocodile. When at last the magic draft was ready, it looked like the clearest water.

"There it is for you," said the witch. Then she cut off the mermaid's tongue, so that she would never again speak or sing. "If the polypi should seize you as you return through the wood," said the witch, "throw over them a few drops of the potion, and their fingers will be torn into a thousand pieces." But the little mermaid had no occasion to do this, for the polypi sprang back in terror when they caught sight of the glittering draft, which shone in her hand like a twinkling star.

So she passed quickly through the wood and the marsh and between the rushing whirlpools. She saw that in her father's palace the torches in the ballroom were extinguished and that all within were asleep. But she did not venture to go in to them, for now that she was dumb and going to leave them forever she felt as if her heart would break. She stole into the garden, took a flower from the flower bed of each of her sisters, kissed her hand towards the palace a thousand times, and then rose up through the dark-blue waters.

The sun had not risen when she came in sight of the prince's palace and approached the beautiful marble steps, but the moon shone clear and bright. Then the little mermaid drank the magic draft, and it seemed as if a two-edged sword went through her delicate body. She fell into a swoon and lay like one dead. When the sun rose and shone over the sea, she recovered and felt a sharp pain, but before her stood the handsome young prince.

"When the sun rose and shone over the sea, she recovered and felt a sharp pain, but before her stood the handsome young prince."

He fixed his coal-black eyes upon her so earnestly that she cast down her own and then became aware that her fish's tail was gone and that she had as pretty a pair of white legs and tiny feet as any little maiden could have. But she had no clothes, so she wrapped herself in her long, thick hair. The prince asked her who she was and whence she came. She looked at him mildly and sorrowfully with her deep blue eyes, but could not speak. He took her by the hand and led her to the palace.

Every step she took was as the witch had said it would be; she felt as if she were treading upon the points of needles or sharp knives. She bore it willingly, however, and moved at the prince's side as lightly as a bubble, so that he and all who saw her wondered at her graceful, swaying movements. She was very soon arrayed in costly robes of silk and muslin and was the most beautiful creature in the palace; but she was dumb and could neither speak nor sing.

Beautiful female slaves, dressed in silk and gold, stepped forward and sang before the prince and his royal parents. One sang better than all the others, and the prince clapped his hands and smiled at her. This was a great sorrow to the little mermaid, for she knew how much more sweetly she herself once could sing, and she thought, "Oh, if he could only know that I have given away my voice forever, to be with him!"

The slaves next performed some pretty fairy-like dances, to the sound of beautiful music. Then the little mermaid raised her lovely white arms, stood on the tips of her toes, glided over the floor, and danced as no one yet had been able to dance. At each moment her beauty was more revealed, and her expressive eyes appealed more directly to the heart than the songs of the slaves. Every one was enchanted, especially the prince, who called her his little foundling. She danced again quite readily, to please him, though each time her foot touched the floor it seemed as if she trod on sharp knives.

The prince said she should remain with him always, and she was given permission to sleep at his door, on a velvet cushion. He had a page's dress made for her, that she might accompany him on horseback. They rode together through the sweet-scented woods, where the green boughs touched their shoulders, and the little birds sang among the fresh leaves. She climbed with him to the tops of high mountains, and although her tender feet bled so that even her steps were marked, she only smiled, and followed him till they could see the clouds beneath them like a flock of birds flying to distant lands. While at the prince's palace, and when all the household were asleep, she would go and sit on the broad marble steps, for it eased her burning feet to bathe them in the cold sea water. It was then that she thought of all those below in the deep.

Once during the night her sisters came up arm in arm, singing sorrowfully as they floated on the water. She beckoned to them, and they recognized her and told her how she had grieved them; after that, they came to the same place every night. Once she saw in the distance her old grandmother, who had not been to the surface of the sea for many years, and the old Sea King, her father, with his crown on his head. They stretched out their hands towards her, but did not venture so near the land as her sisters had.

As the days passed she loved the prince more dearly, and he loved her as one would love a little child. The thought never came to him to make her his wife. Yet unless he married her, she could not receive an immortal soul, and on the morning after his marriage with another, she would dissolve into the foam of the sea.

"Do you not love me the best of them all?" the eyes of the little mermaid seemed to say when he took her in his arms and kissed her fair forehead.

"She would go and sit on the broad marble steps, for it eased her burning feet to bathe them in the cold sea water."

"Yes, you are dear to me," said the prince, "for you have the best heart and you are the most devoted to me. You are like a young maiden whom I once saw, but whom I shall never meet again. I was in a ship that was wrecked, and the waves cast me ashore near a holy temple where several young maidens performed the service. The youngest of them found me on the shore and saved my life. I saw her but twice, and she is the only one in the world whom I could love. But you are like her, and you have almost driven her image from my mind. She belongs to the holy temple, and good fortune has sent you to me in her stead. We will never part.

"Ah, he knows not that it was I who saved his life," thought the little mermaid. "I carried him over the sea to the wood where the temple stands; I sat beneath the foam and watched till the human beings came to help him. I saw the pretty maiden that he loves better than he loves me." The mermaid sighed deeply, but she could not weep. "He says the maiden belongs to the holy temple, therefore she will never return to the world—they will meet no more. I am by his side and see him every day. I will take care of him, and love him, and give up my life for his sake."

Very soon it was said that the prince was to marry and that the beautiful daughter of a neighboring king would be his wife, for a fine ship was being fitted out. Although the prince gave out that he intended merely to pay a visit to the king, it was generally supposed that he went to court the princess. A great company were to go with him. The little mermaid smiled and shook her head. She knew the prince's thoughts better than any of the others.

"Then he kissed her rosy mouth, played with her long, waving hair."

"I must travel," he had said to her; "I must see this beautiful princess. My parents desire it, but they will not oblige me to bring her home as my bride. I cannot love her, because she is not like the beautiful maiden in the temple, whom you resemble. If I were forced to choose a bride, I would choose you, my dumb foundling, with those expressive eyes." Then he kissed her rosy mouth, played with her long, waving hair, and laid his head on her heart, while she dreamed of human happiness and an immortal soul.

"You are not afraid of the sea, my dumb child, are you?" he said, as they stood on the deck of the noble ship which was to carry them to the country of the neighboring king. Then he told her of storm and of calm, of strange fishes in the deep beneath them, and of what the divers had seen there. She smiled at his descriptions, for she knew better than anyone what wonders were at the bottom of the sea.

In the moonlight night, when all on board were asleep except the man at the helm, she sat on deck, gazing down through the clear water. She thought she could distinguish her father's castle, and upon it her aged grandmother, with the silver crown on her head, looking through the rushing tide at the keel of the vessel. Then her sisters came up on the waves and gazed at her mournfully, wringing their white hands. She beckoned to them, and smiled, and wanted to tell them how happy and well off she was. But the cabin boy approached, and when her sisters dived down, he thought what he saw was only the foam of the sea.

The next morning the ship sailed into the harbor of a beautiful town belonging to the king whom the prince was going to visit. The church bells were ringing, and from the high towers sounded a flourish of trumpets. Soldiers, with flying colors and glittering bayonets, lined the roads through which they passed. Every day was a festival, balls and entertainments following one another. But the princess had not yet appeared. People said that she had been brought up and educated in a religious house, where she was learning every royal virtue.

At last she came. Then the little mermaid, who was anxious to see whether she was really beautiful, was obliged to admit that she had never seen a more perfect vision of beauty. Her skin was delicately fair, and beneath her long, dark eyelashes her laughing blue eyes shone with truth and purity.

"It was you," said the prince, "who saved my life when I lay as if dead on the beach," and he folded his blushing bride in his arms.

"Oh, I am too happy!" said he to the little mermaid; "my fondest hopes are now fulfilled. You will rejoice at my happiness, for your devotion to me is great and sincere."

The little mermaid kissed his hand and felt as if her heart were already broken. His wedding morning would bring death to her, and she would change into the foam of the sea.

All the church bells rang, and the heralds rode through the town proclaiming the betrothal. Perfumed oil was burned in costly silver lamps on every altar. The priests waved the censers, while the bride and the bridegroom joined their hands and received the blessing of the bishop. The little mermaid, dressed in silk and gold, held up the bride's train; but her ears heard nothing of the festive music, and her eyes saw not the holy ceremony. She thought of the night of death which was coming to her, and of all she had lost in the world.

On the same evening the bride and bridegroom went on board the ship. Cannons were roaring, flags waving, and in the center of the ship a costly tent of purple and gold had been erected. It contained elegant sleeping couches for the bridal pair during the night. The ship, under a favorable wind, with swelling sails, glided away smoothly and lightly over the calm sea.

When it grew dark, a number of colored lamps were lighted and the sailors danced merrily on the deck. The little mermaid could not help thinking of her first rising out of the sea, when she had seen similar joyful festivities, so she too joined in the dance, poised herself in the air as a swallow when he pursues his prey, and all present cheered her wonderingly. She had never danced so gracefully before. Her tender feet felt as if cut with sharp knives, but she cared not for the pain; a sharper pang had pierced her heart.

She knew this was the last evening she should ever see the prince for whom she had forsaken her kindred and her home. She had given up her beautiful voice and suffered unheard-of pain daily for him, while he knew nothing of it. This was the last evening that she should breathe the same air with him or gaze on the starry sky and the deep sea. An eternal night, without a thought or a dream, awaited her. She had no soul, and now could never win one.

All was joy and gaiety on the ship until long after midnight. She smiled and danced with the rest, while the thought of death was in her heart. The prince kissed his beautiful bride and she played with his raven hair till they went arm in arm to rest in the sumptuous tent. Then all became still on board the ship, and only the pilot, who stood at the helm, was awake. The little mermaid leaned her white arms on the edge of the vessel and looked towards the east for the first blush of morning—for that first ray of the dawn which was to be her death. She saw her sisters rising out of the flood. They were as pale as she, but their beautiful hair no longer waved in the wind; it had been cut off.

"She saw her sisters rising out of the flood. They were as pale as she, but their beautiful hair no longer waved in the wind; it had been cut off."

"We have given our hair to the witch," said they, "to obtain help for you, that you may not die to-night. She has given us a knife; see, it is very sharp. Before the sun rises you must plunge it into the heart of the prince. When the warm blood falls upon your feet they will grow together again into a fish's tail, and you will once more be a mermaid and can return to us to live out your three hundred years before you are changed into the salt sea foam. Haste, then; either he or you must die before sunrise. Our old grandmother mourns so for you that her white hair is falling, as ours fell under the witch's scissors. Kill the prince, and come back. Hasten! Do you not see the first red streaks in the sky? In a few minutes the sun will rise, and you must die."

Then they sighed deeply and mournfully, and sank beneath the waves.

The little mermaid drew back the crimson curtain of the tent and beheld the fair bride, whose head was resting on the prince's breast. She bent down and kissed his noble brow, then looked at the sky, on which the rosy dawn grew brighter and brighter. She glanced at the sharp knife and again fixed her eyes on the prince, who whispered the name of his bride in his dreams.

She was in his thoughts, and the knife trembled in the hand of the little mermaid—but she flung it far from her into the waves. The water turned red where it fell, and the drops that spurted up looked like blood. She cast one more lingering, half-fainting glance at the prince, then threw herself from the ship into the sea and felt her body dissolving into foam.

The sun rose above the waves, and his warm rays fell on the cold foam of the little mermaid, who did not feel as if she were dying. She saw the bright sun, and hundreds of transparent, beautiful creatures floating around her—she could see through them the white sails of the ships and the red clouds in the sky. Their speech was melodious, but could not be heard by mortal ears—just as their bodies could not be seen by mortal eyes. The little mermaid perceived that she had a body like theirs and that she continued to rise higher and higher out of the foam. "Where am I?" asked she, and her voice sounded ethereal, like the voices of those who were with her. No earthly music could imitate it.

"Then threw herself from the ship into the sea and felt her body dissolving into foam."

"Among the daughters of the air," answered one of them. "A mermaid has not an immortal soul, nor can she obtain one unless she wins the love of a human being. On the will of another hangs her eternal destiny. But the daughters of the air, although they do not possess an immortal soul, can, by their good deeds, procure one for themselves. We fly to warm countries and cool the sultry air that destroys mankind with the pestilence. We carry the perfume of the flowers to spread health and restoration.

"After we have striven for three hundred years to do all the good in our power, we receive an immortal soul and take part in the happiness of mankind. You, poor little mermaid, have tried with your whole heart to do as we are doing. You have suffered and endured, and raised yourself to the spirit world by your good deeds, and now, by striving for three hundred years in the same way, you may obtain an immortal soul."

The little mermaid lifted her glorified eyes toward the sun and, for the first time, felt them filling with tears.

On the ship in which she had left the prince there were life and noise, and she saw him and his beautiful bride searching for her. Sorrowfully they gazed at the pearly foam, as if they knew she had thrown herself into the waves. Unseen she kissed the forehead of the bride and fanned the prince, and then mounted with the other children of the air to a rosy cloud that floated above.

"After three hundred years, thus shall we float into the kingdom of heaven," said she. "And we may even get there sooner," whispered one of her companions. "Unseen we can enter the houses of men where there are children, and for every day on which we find a good child that is the joy of his parents and deserves their love, our time of probation is shortened. The child does not know, when we fly through the room, that we smile with joy at his good conduct—for we can count one year less of our three hundred years. But when we see a naughty or a wicked child we shed tears of sorrow, and for every tear a day is added to our time of trial."

The Golden Mermaid

ANDREW LANG

ILLUSTRATIONS HENRY J. FORD

A powerful king had, among many other treasures, a wonderful tree in his garden, which bore every year beautiful golden apples. But the King was never able to enjoy his treasure, for he might watch and guard them as he liked, as soon as they began to get ripe they were always stolen. At last, in despair, he sent for his three sons, and said to the two eldest, "Get yourselves ready for a journey. Take gold and silver with you, and a large retinue of servants, as beseems two noble princes, and go through the world till you find out who it is that steals my golden apples,

49

and, if possible, bring the thief to me that I may punish him as he deserves."

His sons were delighted at this proposal, for they had long wished to see something of the world, so they got ready for their journey with all haste, bade their father farewell, and left the town.

The youngest Prince was much disappointed that he too was not sent out on his travels; but his father wouldn't hear of his going, for he had always been looked upon as the stupid one of the family, and the King was afraid of something happening to him. But the Prince begged and implored so long, that at last his father consented to let him go, and furnished him with gold and silver as he had done his brothers. But he gave him the most wretched horse in his stable, because the foolish youth hadn't asked for a better. So he too set out on his journey to secure the thief, amid the jeers and laughter of the whole court and town.

His path led him first through a wood, and he hadn't gone very far when he met a lean-looking wolf who stood still as he approached. The Prince asked him if he were hungry, and when the wolf said he was, he got down from his horse and said, "If you are really as you say and look, you may take my horse and eat it."

The wolf didn't wait to have the offer repeated, but set to work, and soon made an end of the poor beast.

When the Prince saw how different the wolf looked when he had finished his meal, he said to him, "Now, my friend, since you have eaten up my horse, and I have such a long way to go, that, with the best will in the world, I couldn't manage it on foot, the least you can do for me is to act as my horse and to take me on your back."

"Most certainly," said the wolf, and, letting the Prince mount him, he trotted gaily through the wood. After they had gone a little way he turned round and asked his rider where he wanted to go to, and the Prince proceeded to tell him the whole story of the golden apples that had been stolen out of the King's garden, and how his other two brothers had set forth with many followers to find the thief. When he had finished his story, the wolf, who was in reality no wolf but a mighty magician, said he thought he could tell him who the thief was, and could help him to secure him.

"There lives," he said, "in a neighbouring country, a mighty emperor who has a beautiful golden bird in a cage, and this is the creature who steals the golden apples, but it flies so fast that it is impossible to catch it at its theft. You must slip into the Emperor's palace by night and steal the bird with the cage; but be very careful not to touch the walls as you go out."

The following night the Prince stole into the Emperor's palace, and found the bird in its cage as the wolf had told him he would. He took hold of it carefully, but in spite of all his caution he touched the wall in trying to pass by some sleeping watchmen. They awoke at once, and, seizing him, beat him and put him into chains. Next day he was led before the Emperor, who at once condemned him to death and to be thrown into a dark dungeon till the day of his execution arrived.

The wolf, who, of course, knew by his magic arts all that had happened to the Prince, turned himself at once into a mighty monarch with a large train of followers, and proceeded to the Court of the Emperor, where he was received with every show of honour. The Emperor and he conversed on many subjects, and, among other things, the stranger asked his host if he had many slaves. The Emperor told him he had more than he knew what to do with, and that a new one had been captured that very night for trying to steal his magic bird, but that as he had already more than enough to feed and support, he was going to have this last captive hanged next morning.

"He must have been a most daring thief," said the King, 'to try and steal the magic bird, for depend upon it the creature must have been well guarded. I would really like to see this bold rascal.'

"By all means," said the Emperor; and he himself led his guest down to the dungeon where the unfortunate Prince was kept prisoner. When the Emperor stepped out of the cell with the King, the latter turned to him and said, "Most mighty Emperor, I have been much disappointed. I had thought to find a powerful robber, and instead of that I have seen the most miserable creature I can imagine. Hanging is far too good for him. If I had to sentence him I should make him perform some very difficult task, under pain of death. If he did it so much the better for you, and if he didn't, matters would just be as they are now and he could still be hanged."

"Your counsel," said the Emperor, "is excellent, and, as it happens, I've got the very thing for him to do. My nearest neighbour, who is also a mighty Emperor, possesses a golden horse which he guards most carefully. The prisoner shall be told to steal this horse and bring it to me."

The Prince was then let out of his dungeon, and told his life would be spared if he succeeded in bringing the golden horse to the Emperor. He did not feel very elated at this announcement, for he did not know how in the world he was to set about the task, and he started on his way weeping bitterly, and wondering what had made him leave his father's house and kingdom. But before he had gone far his friend the wolf stood before him and said, "Dear Prince, why are you so cast down? It is true you didn't succeed in catching the bird; but don't let that discourage you, for this time you will be all the more careful, and will doubtless catch the horse."

"When the Emperor stepped out of the cell with the King, the latter turned to him and said."

With these and like words the wolf comforted the Prince, and warned him specially not to touch the wall or let the horse touch it as he led it out, or he would fail in the same way as he had done with the bird.

After a somewhat lengthy journey the Prince and the wolf came to the kingdom ruled over by the Emperor who possessed the golden horse. One evening late they reached the capital, and the wolf advised the Prince to set to work at once, before their presence in the city had aroused the watchfulness of the guards. They slipped unnoticed into the Emperor's stables and into the very place where there were the most guards, for there the wolf rightly surmised they would find the horse. When they came to a certain inner door the wolf told the Prince to remain outside, while he went in.

In a short time he returned and said, "My dear Prince, the horse is most securely watched, but I have bewitched all the guards, and if you will only be careful not to touch the wall yourself, or let the horse touch it as you go out, there is no danger and the game is yours." The Prince, who had made up his mind to be more than cautious this time, went cheerfully to work. He found all the guards fast asleep, and, slipping into the horse's stall, he seized it by the bridle and led it out; but, unfortunately, before they had got quite clear of the stables a gadfly stung the horse and caused it to switch its tail, whereby it touched the wall.

In a moment all the guards awoke, seized the Prince and beat him mercilessly with their horse-whips, after which they bound him with chains, and flung him into a dungeon. Next morning they brought him before the Emperor, who treated him exactly as the King with the golden bird had done, and commanded him to be beheaded on the following day.

When the wolf-magician saw that the Prince had failed this time too, he transformed himself again into a mighty king, and proceeded with an even more gorgeous retinue than the first time to the Court of the Emperor. He was courteously received and entertained, and once more after dinner he led the conversation on to the subject of slaves, and in the course of it again requested to be allowed to see the bold robber who had dared to break into the Emperor's stable to steal his most valuable possession. The Emperor consented, and all happened exactly as it had done at the court of the Emperor with the golden bird; the prisoner's life was to be spared only on condition that within three days he should obtain possession of the golden mermaid, whom hitherto no mortal had ever approached.

Very depressed by his dangerous and difficult task, the Prince left his gloomy prison; but, to his great joy, he met his friend the wolf before he had gone many miles on his journey. The cunning creature pretended he knew nothing of what had happened to the Prince, and asked him how he had fared with the horse. The Prince told him all about his misadventure, and the condition on which the Emperor had promised to spare his life. Then the wolf reminded him that he had twice got him out of prison, and that if he would only trust in him, and do exactly as he told him, he would certainly succeed in this last undertaking. Thereupon they bent their steps towards the sea, which stretched out before them, as far as their eyes could see, all the waves dancing and glittering in the bright sunshine.

"Now," continued the wolf, "I am going to turn myself into a boat full of the most beautiful silken merchandise, and you must jump boldly into the boat, and steer with my tail in your hand right out into the open sea. You will soon come upon the golden mermaid. Whatever you do, don't follow her if she calls you, but on the contrary say to her, "The buyer comes to the seller, not the seller to the buyer." After which you must steer towards the land, and she will follow you, for she won't be able to resist the beautiful wares you have on board your ship."

The Prince promised faithfully to do all he had been told, whereupon the wolf changed himself into a ship full of most exquisite silks, of every shade and colour imaginable. The astonished Prince stepped into the boat, and, holding the wolf's tail in his hand, he steered boldly out into the open sea, where the sun was gilding the blue waves with its golden rays. Soon he saw the golden mermaid swimming near the ship, beckoning and calling to him to follow her; but, mindful of the wolf's warning, he told her in a loud voice that if she wished to buy anything she must come to him. With these words he turned his magic ship round and steered back towards the land.

The mermaid called out to him to stand still, but he refused to listen to her and never paused till he reached the sand of the shore. Here he stopped and waited for the mermaid, who had swum after him. When she drew near the boat he saw that she was far more beautiful than any mortal he had ever beheld. She swam round the ship for some time, and then swung herself gracefully on board, in order to examine the beautiful silken stuffs more closely. Then the Prince seized her in his arms, and kissing her tenderly on the cheeks and lips, he told her she was his forever; at the same moment the boat turned into a wolf again, which so terrified the mermaid that she clung to the Prince for protection.

So the golden mermaid was successfully caught, and she soon felt quite happy in her new life when she saw she had nothing to fear either from the Prince or the wolf—she rode on the back of the latter, and the Prince rode behind her.

When they reached the country ruled over by the Emperor with the golden horse, the Prince jumped down, and, helping the mermaid to alight, he led her before the Emperor. At the sight of the beautiful mermaid and of the grim wolf, who stuck close to the Prince this time, the guards all made respectful obeisance, and soon the three stood before his Imperial Majesty.

When the Emperor heard from the Prince how he had gained possession of his fair prize, he at once recognized that he had been helped by some magic art, and on the spot gave up all claim to the beautiful mermaid. "Dear youth," he said, "forgive me for my shameful conduct to you, and, as a sign that you pardon me, accept the golden horse as a present. I acknowledge your power to be greater even than I can understand, for you have succeeded in gaining possession of the golden mermaid, whom hitherto no mortal has ever been able to approach."

Then they all sat down to a huge feast, and the Prince had to relate his adventures all over again, to the wonder and astonishment of the whole company.

But the Prince was wearying now to return to his own kingdom, so as soon as the feast was over he took farewell of the Emperor, and set out on his homeward way. He lifted the mermaid on to the golden horse, and swung himself up behind her–and so they rode on merrily, with the wolf trotting behind, till they came to the country of the Emperor with the golden bird.

"The Golden Mermaid was caught."

The renown of the Prince and his adventure had gone before him, and the Emperor sat on his throne awaiting the arrival of the Prince and his companions. When the three rode into the courtyard of the palace, they were surprised and delighted to find everything festively illuminated and decorated for their reception. When the Prince and the golden mermaid, with the wolf behind them, mounted the steps of the palace, the Emperor came forward to meet them, and led them to the throne room. At the same moment a servant appeared with the golden bird in its golden cage, and the Emperor begged the Prince to accept it with his love, and to forgive him the indignity he had suffered at his hands. Then the Emperor bent low before the beautiful mermaid, and, offering her his arm, he led her into dinner, closely followed by the Prince and her friend the wolf; the latter seating himself at table, not the least embarrassed that no one had invited him to do so.

As soon as the sumptuous meal was over, the Prince and his mermaid took leave of the Emperor, and, seating themselves on the golden horse, continued their homeward journey. On the way the wolf turned to the Prince and said, "Dear friends, I must now bid you farewell, but I leave you under such happy circumstances that I cannot feel our parting to be a sad one." The Prince was very unhappy when he heard these words, and begged the wolf to stay with them always; but this the good creature refused to do, though he thanked the Prince kindly for his invitation, and called out as he disappeared into the thicket, "Should any evil befall you, dear Prince, at any time, you may rely on my friendship and gratitude." These were the wolf's parting words, and the Prince could not restrain his tears when he saw his friend vanishing in the distance; but one glance at his beloved mermaid soon cheered him up again, and they continued on their journey merrily.

The news of his son's adventures had already reached his father's Court, and everyone was more than astonished at the success of the once despised Prince. His elder brothers, who had in vain gone in pursuit of the thief of the golden apples, were furious over their younger brother's good fortune, and plotted and planned how they were to kill him. They hid themselves in the wood through which the Prince had to pass on his way to the palace, and there fell on him, and, having beaten him to death, they carried off the golden horse and the golden bird. But nothing they could do would persuade the golden mermaid to go with them or move from the spot, for ever since she had left the sea, she had so attached herself to her Prince that she asked nothing else than to live or die with him.

For many weeks the poor mermaid sat and watched over the dead body of her lover, weeping salt tears over his loss, when suddenly one day their old friend the wolf appeared and said, "Cover the Prince's body with all the leaves and flowers you can find in the wood." The maiden did as he told her, and then the wolf breathed over the flowery grave, and, lo and behold! the Prince lay there sleeping as peacefully as a child. "Now you may wake him if you like," said the wolf, and the mermaid bent over him and gently kissed the wounds his brothers had made on his forehead, and the Prince awoke, and you may imagine how delighted he was to find his beautiful mermaid beside him, though he felt a little depressed when he thought of the loss of the golden bird and the golden horse. After a time the wolf, who had likewise fallen on the Prince's neck, advised them to continue their journey, and once more the Prince and his lovely bride mounted on the faithful beast's back.

"'Now you may wake him if you like,' said the wolf"

The King's joy was great when he embraced his youngest son, for he had long since despaired of his return. He received the wolf and the beautiful golden mermaid most cordially too, and the Prince was made to tell his adventures all over from the beginning. The poor old father grew very sad when he heard of the shameful conduct of his elder sons, and had them called before him. They turned as white as death when they saw their brother, whom they thought they had murdered, standing beside them alive and well, and so startled were they that when the King asked them why they had behaved so wickedly to their brother they could think of no lie, but confessed at once that they had slain the young Prince in order to obtain possession of the golden horse and the golden bird. Their father's wrath knew no bounds, and he ordered them both to be banished, but he could not do enough to honour his youngest son, and his marriage with the beautiful mermaid was celebrated with much pomp and magnificence. When the festivities were over, the wolf bade them all farewell, and returned once more to his life in the woods, much to the regret of the old King and the young Prince and his bride.

And so ended the adventures of the Prince with his friend the wolf.

POLAND

The Good Ferryman and the Water Nymphs

MAUDE ASHURT BIGGS
ILLUSTRATIONS IVAN BILIBIN AND CECILE WALTON

T here was once an old man, very poor, with three sons. They lived chiefly by ferrying people over a river; but he had had nothing but ill-luck all his life. And to crown all, on the night he died, there was a great storm, and in it the crazy old ferry-boat, on which his sons depended for a living, was sunk.

As they were lamenting both their father and their poverty, an old man came by, and learning the reason of their sorrow said:

"Never mind; all will come right in time. Look! there is your boat as good as new."

And there was a fine new ferry-boat on the water, in place of the old one, and a number of people waiting to be ferried over.

The three brothers arranged to take turns with the boat, and divide the fares they took.

They were however very different in disposition. The two elder brothers were greedy and avaricious, and would never take anyone over the river, without being handsomely paid for it.

But the youngest brother took over poor people, who had no money, for nothing; and moreover frequently relieved their wants out of his own pocket.

One day, at sunset, when the eldest brother was at the ferry the same old man, who had visited them on the night their father died, came, and asked for a passage.

"I have nothing to pay you with, but this empty purse," he said.

"Go and get something to put in it then first," replied the ferry-man; "and be off with you now!"

Next day it was the second brother's turn; and the same old man came, and offered his empty purse as his fare. But he met with a like reply.

The third day it was the youngest brother's turn; and when the old man arrived, and asked to be ferried over for charity, he answered:

"Yes, get in, old man."

"And what is the fare?" asked the old man.

"That depends upon whether you can pay or not," was the reply; "but if you cannot, it is all the same to me."

"A good deed is never without its reward," said the old man: "but in the meantime take this empty purse; though it is very worn, and looks worth nothing. But if you shake it, and say:

'For his sake who gave it, this purse I hold, I wish may always be full of gold;' it will always afford you as much gold as you wish for."

The youngest brother came home, and his brothers, who were sitting over a good supper, laughed at him, because he had taken only a few copper coins that day, and they told him he should have no supper. But when he began to shake his purse and scatter gold coins all about, they jumped up from the table, and began picking them up eagerly.

The purse that was ever full

And as it was share and share alike, they all grew rich very quickly. The youngest brother made good use of his riches, for he gave away money freely to the poor. But the greedy elder brothers envied him the possession of the wonderful purse, and contrived to steal it from him. Then they left their old home; and the one bought a ship, laded it with all sorts of merchandize, for a trading voyage. But the ship ran upon a rock, and everyone on board was drowned. The second brother was no more fortunate, for as he was travelling through a forest, with an enormous treasure of precious stones, in which he had laid out his wealth, to sell at a profit, he was waylaid by robbers, who murdered him, and shared the spoil among them.

The youngest brother, who remained at home, having lost his purse, became as poor as before. But he still did as formerly, took pay from passengers who could afford it, ferried over poor folks for nothing, and helped those who were poorer than himself so far as he could.

One day the same old man with the long white beard came by; the ferry-man welcomed him as an old friend, and while rowing him over the river, told him all that had happened since he last saw him.

"Your brothers did very wrong, and they have paid for it," said the old man; "but you were in fault yourself. Still, I will give you one more chance. Take this hook and line; and whatever you catch, mind you hold fast, and not let it escape you; or you will bitterly repent it."

The old man then disappeared, and the ferry-man looked in wonder at his new fishing-tackle — a diamond hook, a silver line, and a golden rod.

All at once the hook sprang of itself into the water; the line lengthened out along the river current, and there came a strong pull upon it. The fisherman drew it in, and beheld a most lovely creature, upwards from the waist a woman, but with a fish's tail.

"Good ferry-man, let me go," she said; "take your hook out of my hair! The sun is setting, and after sunset I can no longer be a water-nymph again."

But without answering, the ferry-man only held her fast, and covered her over with his coat, to prevent her escaping. Then the sun set, and she lost her fish-tail.

"Now," she said: "I am yours; so let us go to the nearest church and get married."

She was already dressed as a bride, with a myrtle garland on her head, in a white dress, with a rainbow-coloured girdle, and rich jewels in her hair and on her neck. And she held in her hand the wonderful purse that was always full of gold.

They found the priest and all ready at the church; were married in a few minutes; and then came home to their wedding-feast, to which all the neighbours were invited. They were royally entertained, and when they were about to leave the bride shook the wonderful purse, and sent a shower of gold pieces flying among the guests; so they all went home very well pleased.

The good ferry-man and his marvellous wife lived most happily together; they never wanted for anything, and gave freely to all who came. He continued to ply his ferry-boat; but he now took all passengers over for nothing, and gave them each a piece of gold into the bargain.

Now there was a king over that country, who a year ago had just succeeded to his elder brother. He had heard of the ferry-man, who was so marvellously rich, and wishing to ascertain the truth of the story he had heard, came on purpose to see for himself. But when he saw the ferry-man's beautiful young wife, he resolved to have her for himself, and determined to get rid of her husband somehow.

At that time there was an eclipse of the sun; and the king sent for the ferry-man, and told him he must find out the cause of this eclipse, or be put to death.

He came home in great distress to his wife; but she replied:

"Never mind, my dear. I will tell you what to do, and how to gratify the king's curiosity."

So she gave him a wonderful ball of thread, which he was to throw before him, and follow the thread as it kept unwinding — towards the East.

He went on a long way, over high mountains, deep rivers, and wide regions. At last he came to a ruined city, where a number of corpses were lying about unburied, tainting the air with pestilence.

The good man was sorry to see this, and took the pains to summon men from the neighbouring cities, and get the bodies properly buried. He then resumed his journey.

He came at last to the ends of the earth. Here he found a magnificent golden palace, with an amber roof, and diamond doors and windows.

The ball of thread went straight into the palace, and the ferry-man found himself in a vast apartment, where sat a very dignified old lady, spinning from a golden distaff.

"Wretched man! what are you here for?" she exclaimed, when she saw him. "My son will come back presently and burn you up."

He explained to her how he had been forced to come, out of sheer necessity.

"Well, I must help you," replied the old lady, who was no less than the Mother of the Sun, "because you did Sol that good turn some days ago, in burying the inhabitants of that town, when they were killed by a dragon. He journeys every day across the wide arch of heaven, in a diamond car, drawn by twelve grey horses, with golden manes, giving heat and light to the whole world. He will soon be back here, to rest for the night.... But ... here he comes; hide yourself, and take care to observe what follows."

So saying she changed her visitor into a lady-bird, and let him fly to the window.

Then the neighing of the wonderful horses and the rattling of chariot wheels were heard, and the bright Sun himself presently came in, and stretching himself upon a coral bed, remarked to his mother:

"I smell a human being here!"

"What nonsense you talk!" replied his mother. "How could any human being come here? You know it is impossible."

The Sun, as if he did not quite believe her, began to peer anxiously about the room.

"Don't be so restless," said the old lady; "but tell me why you suffered eclipse a month or two ago."

"How could I help it?" answered the Sun; "When the dragon from the deep abyss attacked me, and I had to fight him? Perhaps I should have been fighting with the monster till now, if a wonderful mermaid had not come to help me. When she began to sing, and looked at the dragon with her beautiful eyes, all his rage softened at once; he was absorbed in gazing upon her beauty, and I meanwhile burnt him to ashes, and threw them into the sea."

The Sun then went to sleep, and his mother again touched the ferry-man with her spindle; he then returned to his natural shape, and slipped out of the palace. Following the ball of thread he reached home at last, and next day went to the king, and told him all.

But the king was so enchanted at the description of the beautiful sea-maiden, that he ordered the ferry-man to go and bring her to him, on pain of death.

He went home very sad to his wife, but she told him she would manage this also. So saying she gave him another ball of thread, to show him which way to go, and she also gave him a carriage-load of costly lady's apparel and jewels, and ornaments — told him what he was to do, and they took leave of one another.

On the way the ferry-man met a youth, riding on a fine grey horse, who asked:

"What have you got there, man?"

"A woman's wearing apparel, most costly and beautiful" — he had several dresses, not simply one.

"I say, give me some of those as a present for my intended, whom I am going to see. I can be of use to you, for I am the Storm-wind. I will come, whenever you call upon me thus:

'Storm-wind! Storm-wind! come with speed! Help me in my sudden need!' "

The ferry-man gave him some of the most beautiful things he had, and the Storm-wind passed.

A little further on he met an old man, grey-haired, but strong and vigorous-looking, who also said:

"What have you got there?"

"Women's garments costly and beautiful."

"I am going to my daughter's wedding; she is to marry the Storm-wind; give me something as a wedding present for her, and I will be of use to you. I am the Frost; if you need me call upon me thus:

'Frost, I call thee; come with speed; Help me in my sudden need!'"

The ferry-man let him take all he wanted and went on.

And now he came to the sea-coast; here the ball of thread stopped, and would go no further.

The ferry-man waded up to his waist into the sea, and set up two high poles, with cross-bars between them, upon which he hung dresses of various colours, scarves, and ribbons, gold chains, and diamond earrings and pins, shoes, and looking-glasses, and then hid himself, with his wonderful hook and line ready.

As soon as the morning rose from the sea, there appeared far away on the smooth waters a silvery boat, in which stood a beautiful maiden, with a golden oar in one hand, while with the other she gathered together her long golden hair, all the while singing so beautifully to the rising sun, that, if the ferry-man had not quickly stopped his ears, he would have fallen into a delicious reverie, and then asleep.

She sailed along a long time in her silver boat, and round her leaped and played golden fishes with rainbow wings and diamond eyes. But all at once she perceived the rich clothes and ornaments, hung up on the poles, and as she came nearer, the ferry-man called out:

"Storm-wind! Storm-wind! come with speed! Help me in my sudden need!"

"What do you want?" asked the Storm-wind.

The ferry-man without answering him, called out:

"Frost, I call thee; come with speed, Help me in my sudden need!"

"What do you want?" asked the Frost.

The meeting of the sisters

"I want to capture the sea-maiden."

Then the wind blew and blew, so that the silver boat was capsized, and the frost breathed on the sea till it was frozen over.

Then the ferryman rushed up to the sea-maiden, entangling his hook in her golden hair; lifted her on his horse, and rode off as swift as the wind after his wonderful ball of thread.

She kept weeping and lamenting all the way; but as soon as they reached the ferry-man's home, and saw his wife, all her sorrow changed into joy; she laughed with delight, and threw herself into her arms.

And then it turned out that the two were sisters.

Next morning the ferry-man went to court with both his wife and sister-in-law, and the king was so delighted with the beauty of the latter, that he at once offered to marry her. But she could give him no answer until he had the Self-playing Guitar.

So the king ordered the ferry-man to procure him this wonderful guitar, or be put to death.

His wife told him what to do, and gave him a handkerchief of hers, embroidered with gold, telling him to use this in case of need.

Following the ball of thread he came at last to a great lake, in the midst of which was a green island.

He began to wonder how he was to get there, when he saw a boat approaching, in which was an old man, with a long white beard, and he recognized him with delight, as his former benefactor.

"How are you, ferry-man?" he asked. "Where are you going?"

"I am going wherever the ball of thread leads me, for I must fetch the Self-playing Guitar."

"This guitar," said the old man, "belongs to Goldmore, the lord of that island. It is a difficult matter to have to do with him; but perhaps you may succeed. You have often ferried me over the water; I will ferry you now."

The old man pushed off, and they reached the island.

On arriving the ball of thread went straight into a palace, where Goldmore came out to meet the traveller, and asked him where he was going and what he wanted.

He explained:

"I am come for the Self-playing Guitar."

"I will only let you have it on condition that you do not go to sleep for three days and nights. And if you do, you will not only lose all chance of the Self-playing Guitar; but you must die."

What could the poor man do, but agree to this?

So Goldmore conducted him to a great room, and locked him in. The floor was strewn with sleepy-grass, so he fell asleep directly.

Next morning in came Goldmore, and on waking him up said:

"So you went to sleep! Very well, you shall die!"

And he touched a spring in the floor, and the unhappy ferry-man fell down into an apartment beneath, where the walls were of looking-glass, and there were great heaps of gold and precious stones lying about.

For three days and nights he lay there; he was fearfully hungry. And then it dawned upon him that he was to be starved to death!

He called out, and entreated in vain; nobody answered, and though he had piles of gold and jewels about him, they could not purchase him a morsel of food.

He sought in vain for any means of exit. There was a window, of clearest crystal, but it was barred by a heavy iron grating. But the window looked into a garden whence he could hear nightingales singing, doves cooing, and the murmur of a brook. But inside he saw only heaps of useless gold and jewels, and his own face, worn and haggard, reflected a thousand times.

He could now only pray for a speedy death, and took out a little iron cross, which he had kept by him since his boyhood. But in doing so he also drew out the gold-embroidered handkerchief, given him by his wife, and which he had quite forgotten till now.

Goldmore had been looking on, as he often did, from an opening in the ceiling to enjoy the sight of his prisoner's sufferings. All at once he recognized the handkerchief, as belonging to his own sister, the ferry-man's wife.

He at once changed his treatment of his brother-in-law, as he had discovered him to be; took him out of prison, led him to his own apartments, gave him food and drink, and the Self-playing Guitar into the bargain.

Coming home, the ferry-man met his wife half-way.

"The ball of thread came home alone," she explained; "so I judged that some misfortune had befallen you, and I was coming to help you."

He told her all his adventures, and they returned home together.

The king was all eagerness to see and hear the Self-playing Guitar; so he ordered the ferry-man, his wife, and her sister to come with it to the palace at once.

Now the property of this Self-playing Guitar was such that wherever its music was heard, the sick became well, those who were sad merry, ugly folks became handsome, sorceries were dissolved, and those who had been murdered rose from the dead, and slew their murderers.

So when the king, having been told the charm to set the guitar playing, said the words, all the court began to be merry, and dance — except the king himself!... For all at once the door opened, the music ceased, and the figure of the late king stood up in his shroud, and said:

"I was the rightful possessor of the throne! and you, wicked brother, who caused me to be murdered, shall now reap your reward!"

So saying he breathed upon him, and the king fell dead — on which the phantom vanished.

But as soon as they recovered from their fright, all the nobility who were present acclaimed the ferry-man as their king.

The next day, after the burial of the late king, the beautiful sea-maiden, the beloved of the Sun, went back to the sea, to float about in her silvery canoe, in the company of the rainbow fishes, and to rejoice in the sunbeams.

But the good ferry-man and his wife lived happily ever after, as king and queen. And they gave a grand ball to the nobility and to the people.... The Self-playing Guitar furnished the music, the wonderful purse scattered gold all the time, and the king entertained all the guests right royally.

SCOTLAND

The Mermaid Wife

CHARLES JOHN TIBBITS
ILLUSTRATIONS KARL WILHELM DIEFENBACH

A story is told of an inhabitant of Unst, who, in walking on the sandy margin of a voe, saw a number of mermen and mermaids dancing by moonlight, and several seal-skins strewed beside them on the ground. At his approach they immediately fled to secure their garbs, and, taking upon themselves the form of seals, plunged immediately into the sea. But as the Shetlander perceived that one skin lay close to his feet, he snatched it up, bore it swiftly away, and placed it in concealment. On returning to the shore he met the fairest damsel that was ever gazed upon by mortal eyes, lamenting the robbery, by which she had become an exile from her submarine friends, and a tenant of the upper world.

Vainly she implored the restitution of her property; the man had drunk deeply of love, and was inexorable; but he offered her protection beneath his roof as his betrothed spouse. The merlady, perceiving that she must become an inhabitant of the earth, found that she could not do better than accept of the offer. This strange attachment subsisted for many years, and the couple had several children. The Shetlander's love for his merwife was unbounded, but his affection was coldly returned.

The lady would often steal alone to the desert strand, and, on a signal being given, a large seal would make his appearance, with whom she would hold, in an unknown tongue, an anxious conference. Years had thus glided away, when it happened that one of the children, in the course of his play, found concealed beneath a stack of corn a seal's skin; and, delighted with the prize, he ran with it to his mother. Her eyes glistened with rapture — she gazed upon it as her own—as the means by which she could pass through the ocean that led to her native home. She burst forth into an ecstasy of joy, which was only moderated when she beheld her children, whom she was now about to leave; and, after hastily embracing them, she fled with all speed towards the sea-side.

The husband immediately returned, learned the discovery that had taken place, ran to overtake his wife, but only arrived in time to see her transformation of shape completed — to see her, in the form of a seal, bound from the ledge of a rock into the sea. The large animal of the same kind with whom she had held a secret converse soon appeared, and evidently congratulated her, in the most tender manner, on her escape. But before she dived to unknown depths, she cast a parting glance at the wretched Shetlander, whose despairing looks excited in her breast a few transient feelings of commiseration.

"Farewell!" said she to him, "and may all good attend you. I loved you very well when I resided upon earth, but I always loved my first husband much better."

The Girl-Fish

ANDREW LANG,
FROM THE ORIGINAL BY FRANCISCO MASPONS Y LABRÓS
ILLUSTRATIONS HENRY J. FORD

O nce upon a time there lived, on the bank of a stream, a man and a woman who had a daughter. As she was an only child, and very pretty besides, they never could make up their minds to punish her for her faults or to teach her nice manners; and as for work– she laughed in her mother's face if she asked her to help cook the dinner or to wash the plates. All the girl would do was to spend her days in dancing and playing with her friends; and for any use she was to her parents they might as well have no daughter at all.

However, one morning her mother looked so tired that even the selfish girl could not help seeing it, and asked if there was anything she was able to do, so that her mother might rest a little.

The good woman looked so surprised and grateful for this offer that the girl felt rather ashamed, and at that moment would have scrubbed down the house if she had been requested; but her mother only begged her to take the fishing-net out to the bank of the river and mend some holes in it, as her father intended to go fishing that night.

The girl took the net and worked so hard that soon there was not a hole to be found. She felt quite pleased with herself, though she had had plenty to amuse her, as everybody who passed by had stopped and had a chat with her. But by this time the sun was high overhead, and she was just folding her net to carry it home again, when she heard a splash behind her, and looking round she saw a big fish jump into the air. Seizing the net with both hands, she flung it into the water where the circles were spreading one behind the other, and, more by luck than skill, drew out the fish.

"Well, you are a beauty!" she cried to herself; but the fish looked up to her and said:

"You had better not kill me, for, if you do, I will turn you into a fish yourself!"

The girl laughed contemptuously, and ran straight in to her mother.

"Look what I have caught," she said gaily; "but it is almost a pity to eat it, for it can talk, and it declares that, if I kill it, it will turn me into a fish too."

"Oh, put it back, put it back!" implored the mother. "Perhaps it is skilled in magic. And I should die, and so would your father, if anything should happen to you."

"Oh, nonsense, mother; what power could a creature like that have over me? Besides, I am hungry, and if I don't have my dinner soon, I shall be cross." And off she went to gather some flowers to stick in her hair.

About an hour later the blowing of a horn told her that dinner was ready.

"Didn't I say that fish would be delicious?" she cried; and plunging her spoon into the dish the girl helped herself to a large piece. But the instant it touched her mouth a cold shiver ran through her. Her head seemed to flatten, and her eyes to look oddly round the corners; her legs and her arms were stuck to her sides, and she gasped wildly for breath. With a mighty bound she sprang through the window and fell into the river, where she soon felt better, and was able to swim to the sea, which was close by.

No sooner had she arrived there than the sight of her sad face attracted the notice of some of the other fishes, and they pressed round her, begging her to tell them her story.

"I am not a fish at all," said the new-comer, swallowing a great deal of salt water as she spoke; for you cannot learn how to be a proper fish all in a moment. "I am not a fish at all, but a girl; at least I was a girl a few minutes ago, only–" And she ducked her head under the waves so that they should not see her crying.

"Only you did not believe that the fish you caught had power to carry out its threat," said an old tunny. "Well, never mind, that has happened to all of us, and it really is not a bad life. Cheer up and come with us and see our queen, who lives in a palace that is much more beautiful than any your queens can boast of."

The new fish felt a little afraid of taking such a journey; but as she was still more afraid of being left alone, she waved her tail in token of consent, and off they all set, hundreds of them together. The people on the rocks and in the ships that saw them pass said to each other:

"Look what a splendid shoal!" and had no idea that they were hastening to the queen's palace; but, then, dwellers on land have so little notion of what goes on in the bottom of the sea! Certainly the little new fish had none. She had watched jelly-fish and nautilus swimming a little way below the surface, and beautiful coloured sea-weeds floating about; but that was all. Now, when she plunged deeper her eyes fell upon strange things.

Wedges of gold, great anchors, heaps of pearl, inestimable stones, unvalued jewels – all scattered in the bottom of the sea! Dead men's bones were there also, and long white creatures who had never seen the light, for they mostly dwelt in the clefts of rocks where the sun's rays could not come. At first our little fish felt as if she were blind also, but by-and-by she began to make out one object after another in the green dimness, and by the time she had swum for a few hours all became clear.

"Here we are at last," cried a big fish, going down into a deep valley, for the sea has its mountains and valleys just as much as the land. "That is the palace of the queen of the fishes, and I think you must confess that the emperor himself has nothing so fine."

"It is beautiful indeed," gasped the little fish, who was very tired with trying to swim as fast as the rest, and beautiful beyond words the palace was. The walls were made of pale pink coral, worn smooth by the waters, and round the windows were rows of pearls; the great doors were standing open, and the whole troop floated into the chamber of audience, where the queen, who was half a woman after all, was seated on a throne made of a green and blue shell.

"Who are you, and where do you come from?" said she to the little fish, whom the others had pushed in front. And in a low, trembling voice, the visitor told her story.

"I was once a girl too," answered the queen, when the fish had ended; "and my father was the king of a great country. A husband was found for me, and on my wedding day my mother placed her crown on my head and told me that as long as I wore it I should likewise be queen. For many months I was as happy as a girl could be, especially when I had a little son to play with. But, one morning, when I was walking in my gardens, there came a giant and snatched the crown from my head. Holding me fast, he told me that he intended to give the crown to his daughter, and to enchant my husband the prince, so that he should not know the difference between us. Since then she has filled my place and been queen in my stead. As for me, I was so miserable that I threw myself into the sea, and my ladies, who loved me, declared that they would die too; but, instead of dying, some wizard, who pitied my fate, turned us all into fishes, though he allowed me to keep the face and body of a woman. And fished we must remain till someone brings me back my crown again!"

"I will bring it back if you tell me what to do!" cried the little fish, who would have promised anything that was likely to carry her up to earth again. And the queen answered:

"Yes, I will tell you what to do."

She sat silent for a moment, and then went on:

"There is no danger if you will only follow my counsel; and first you must return to earth, and go up to the top of a high mountain, where the giant has built his castle. You will find him sitting on the steps weeping for his daughter, who has just died while the prince was away hunting. At the last she sent her father my crown by a faithful servant. But I warn you to be careful, for if he sees you he may kill you. Therefore I will give you the power to change yourself into any creature that may help you best. You have only to strike your forehead, and call out its name."

This time the journey to land seemed much shorter than before, and when once the fish reached the shore she struck her forehead sharply with her tail, and cried:

"Deer, come to me!"

In a moment the small, slimy body disappeared, and in its place stood a beautiful beast with branching horns and slender legs, quivering with longing to be gone. Throwing back her head and snuffing the air, she broke into a run, leaping easily over the rivers and walls that stood in her way.

It happened that the king's son had been hunting since daybreak, but had killed nothing, and when the deer crossed his path as he was resting under a tree he determined to have her. He flung himself on his horse, which went like the wind, and as the prince had often hunted the forest before, and knew all the short cuts, he at last came up with the panting beast.

"By your favour let me go, and do not kill me," said the deer, turning to the prince with tears in her eyes, "for I have far to run and much to do." And as the prince, struck dumb with surprise, only looked at her, the deer cleared the next wall and was soon out of sight.

"That can't really be a deer," thought the prince to himself, reining in his horse and not attempting to follow her. "No deer ever had eyes like that. It must be an enchanted maiden, and I will marry her and no other." So, turning his horse's head, he rode slowly back to his palace.

The deer reached the giant's castle quite out of breath, and her heart sank as she gazed at the tall, smooth walls which surrounded it. Then she plucked up courage and cried:

"Ant, come to me!" And in a moment the branching horns and beautiful shape had vanished, and a tiny brown ant, invisible to all who did not look closely, was climbing up the walls.

It was wonderful how fast she went, that little creature! The wall must have appeared miles high in comparison with her own body; yet, in less time than would have seemed possible, she was over the top and down in the courtyard on the other side. Here she paused to consider what had best be done next, and looking about her she saw that one of the walls had a tall tree growing by it, and in the corner was a window very nearly on a level with the highest branches of the tree.

"Monkey, come to me!" cried the ant; and before you could turn round a monkey was swinging herself from the topmost branches into the room where the giant lay snoring.

"Perhaps he will be so frightened at the sight of me that he may die of fear, and I shall never get the crown," thought the monkey. "I had better become something else." And she called softly: "Parrot, come to me!"

Then a pink and grey parrot hopped up to the giant, who by this time was stretching himself and giving yawns which shook the castle. The parrot waited a little, until he was really awake, and then she said boldly that she had been sent to take away the crown, which was not his any longer, now his daughter the queen was dead.

On hearing these words the giant leapt out of bed with an angry roar, and sprang at the parrot in order to wring her neck with his great hands. But the bird was too quick for him, and, flying behind his back, begged the giant to have patience, as her death would be of no use to him.

"That is true," answered the giant; "but I am not so foolish as to give you that crown for nothing. Let me think what I will have in exchange!" And he scratched his huge head for several minutes, for giants' minds always move slowly.

"Ah, yes, that will do!" exclaimed the giant at last, his face brightening. "You shall have the crown if you will bring me a collar of blue stones from the Arch of St. Martin, in the Great City."

Now when the parrot had been a girl she had often heard of this wonderful arch and the precious stones and marbles that had been let into it. It sounded as if it would be a very hard thing to get them away from the building of which they formed a part, but all had gone well with her so far, and at any rate she could but try. So she bowed to the giant, and made her way back to the window where the giant could not see her. Then she called quickly:

"Eagle, come to me!"

Before she had even reached the tree she felt herself borne up on strong wings ready to carry her to the clouds if she wished to go there, and seeming a mere speck in the sky, she was swept along till she beheld the Arch of St. Martin far below, with the rays of the sun shining on it. Then she swooped down, and, hiding herself behind a buttress so that she could not be detected from below, she set herself to dig out the nearest blue stones with her beak. It was even harder work than she had expected; but at last it was done, and hope arose in her heart. She next drew out a piece of string that she had found hanging from a tree, and sitting down to rest strung the stones together. When the necklace was finished she hung it round her neck, and called: "Parrot, come to me!" And a little later the pink and grey parrot stood before the giant.

"Here is the necklace you asked for," said the parrot. And the eyes of the giant glistened as he took the heap of blue stones in his hand. But for all that he was not minded to give up the crown.

"They are hardly as blue as I expected," he grumbled, though the parrot knew as well as he did that he was not speaking the truth; "so you must bring me something else in exchange for the crown you covet so much. If you fail it will cost you not only the crown but you life also."

"What is it you want now?" asked the parrot; and the giant answered:

"If I give you my crown I must have another still more beautiful; and this time you shall bring me a crown of stars."

The parrot turned away, and as soon as she was outside she murmured:

"Toad, come to me!" And sure enough a toad she was, and off she set in search of the starry crown.

She had not gone far before she came to a clear pool, in which the stars were reflected so brightly that they looked quite real to touch and handle. Stooping down she filled a bag she was carrying with the shining water and, returning to the castle, wove a crown out of the reflected stars. Then she cried as before:

"Parrot, come to me!" And in the shape of a parrot she entered the presence of the giant.

"Here is the crown you asked for," she said; and this time the giant could not help crying out with admiration. He knew he was beaten, and still holding the chaplet of stars, he turned to the girl.

"Your power is greater than mine: take the crown; you have won it fairly!"

The parrot did not need to be told twice. Seizing the crown, she sprang on to the window, crying: "Monkey, come to me!" And to a monkey, the climb down the tree into the courtyard did not take half a minute. When she had reached the ground she said again: "Ant, come to me!" And a little ant at once began to crawl over the high wall. How glad the ant was to be out of the giant's castle, holding fast the crown which had shrunk into almost nothing, as she herself had done, but grew quite big again when the ant exclaimed:

"Deer, come to me!"

Surely no deer ever ran so swiftly as that one! On and on she went, bounding over rivers and crashing through tangles till she reached the sea. Here she cried for the last time:

"Fish, come to me!" And, plunging in, she swam along the bottom as far as the palace, where the queen and all the fishes gathered together awaiting her.

The hours since she had left had gone very slowly–as they always do to people that are waiting–and many of them had quite given up hope.

"I am tired of staying here," grumbled a beautiful little creature, whose colours changed with every movement of her body, "I want to see what is going on in the upper world. It must be months since that fish went away."

"It was a very difficult task, and the giant must certainly have killed her or she would have been back long ago," remarked another.

"The young flies will be coming out now," murmured a third, 'and they will all be eaten up by the river fish! It is really too bad!" When, suddenly, a voice was heard from behind: "Look! look! what is that bright thing that is moving so swiftly towards us?" And the queen started up, and stood on her tail, so excited was she.

A silence fell on all the crowd, and even the grumblers held their peace and gazed like the rest. On and on came the fish, holding the crown tightly in her mouth, and the others moved back to let her pass. On she went right up to the queen, who bent and, taking the crown, placed it on her own head. Then a wonderful thing happened. Her tail dropped away or, rather, it divided and grew into two legs and a pair of the prettiest feet in the world, while her maidens, who were grouped around her, shed their scales and became girls again. They all turned and looked at each other first, and next at the little fish who had regained her own shape and was more beautiful than any of them.

"It is you who have given us back our life; you, you!" they cried; and fell to weeping from very joy.

So they all went back to earth and the queen's palace, and quite forgot the one that lay under the sea. But they had been so long away that they found many changes. The prince, the queen's husband, had died some years since, and in his place was her son, who had grown up and was king! Even in his joy at seeing his mother again an air of sadness clung to him, and at last the queen could bear it no longer, and begged him to walk with her in the garden. Seated together in a bower of jessamine–where she had passed long hours as a bride–she took her son's hand and entreated him to tell her the cause of his sorrow. "For," said she, "if I can give you happiness you shall have it."

"It is no use," answered the prince; "nobody can help me. I must bear it alone."

"But at least let me share your grief," urged the queen.

"No one can do that," said he. "I have fallen in love with what I can never marry, and I must get on as best I can."

"It may not be as impossible as you think," answered the queen. "At any rate, tell me."

There was silence between them for a moment, then, turning away his head, the prince answered gently:

"I have fallen in love with a beautiful deer!"

'Ah, if that is all,' exclaimed the queen joyfully. And she told him in broken words that, as he had guessed, it was no deer but an enchanted maiden who had won back the crown and brought her home to her own people.

"She is here, in my palace," added the queen. "I will take you to her."

But when the prince stood before the girl, who was so much more beautiful than anything he had ever dreamed of, he lost all his courage, and stood with bent head before her.

Then the maiden drew near, and her eyes, as she looked at him, were the eyes of the deer that day in the forest. She whispered softly:

"By your favour let me go, and do not kill me."

And the prince remembered her words, and his heart
was filled with happiness. And the queen, his mother,
watched them and smiled.

The Mermaid and the Boy

ANDREW LANG

ILLUSTRATIONS HENRY J. FORD

L ong, long ago, there lived a king who ruled over a country by the sea. When he had been married about a year, some of his subjects, inhabiting a distant group of islands, revolted against his laws, and it became needful for him to leave his wife and go in person to settle their disputes. The queen feared that some ill would come of it, and implored him to stay at home, but he told her that nobody could do his work for him, and the next morning the sails were spread, and the king started on his voyage.

The vessel had not gone very far when she ran upon a rock, and stuck so fast in a cleft that the strength of the whole crew could not get her off again. To make matters worse, the wind was rising too, and it was quite plain that in a few hours the ship would be dashed to pieces and everybody would be drowned, when suddenly the form of a mermaid was seen dancing on the waves which threatened every moment to overwhelm them.

"There is only one way to free yourselves," she said to the king, bobbing up and down in the water as she spoke, "and that is to give me your solemn word that you will deliver to me the first child that is born to you."

The king hesitated at this proposal. He hoped that someday he might have children in his home, and the thought that he must yield up the heir to his crown was very bitter to him; but just then a huge wave broke with great force on the ship's side, and his men fell on their knees and entreated him to save them.

So he promised, and this time a wave lifted the vessel clean off the rocks, and she was in the open sea once more.

The affairs of the islands took longer to settle than the king had expected, and some months passed away before he returned to his palace. In his absence a son had been born to him, and so great was his joy that he quite forgot the mermaid and the price he had paid for the safety of his ship. But as the years went on, and the baby grew into a fine big boy, the remembrance of it came back, and one day he told the queen the whole story. From that moment the happiness of both their lives was ruined. Every night they went to bed wondering if they should find his room empty in the morning, and every day they kept him by their sides, expecting him to be snatched away before their very eyes.

At last the king felt that this state of things could not continue, and he said to his wife:

"After all, the most foolish thing in the world one can do is to keep the boy here in exactly the place in which the mermaid will seek him. Let us give him food and send him on his travels, and perhaps, if the mermaid ever blocs come to seek him, she may be content with some other child." And the queen agreed that his plan seemed the wisest.

So the boy was called, and his father told him the story of the voyage, as he had told his mother before him. The prince listened eagerly, and was delighted to think that he was to go away all by himself to see the world, and was not in the least frightened; for though he was now sixteen, he had scarcely been allowed to walk alone beyond the palace gardens. He began busily to make his preparations, and took off his smart velvet coat, putting on instead one of green cloth, while he refused a beautiful bag which the queen offered him to hold his food, and slung a leather knapsack over his shoulders instead, just as he had seen other travellers do. Then he bade farewell to his parents and went his way.

All through the day he walked, watching with interest the strange birds and animals that darted across his path in the forest or peeped at him from behind a bush. But as evening drew on he became tired, and looked about as he walked for some place where he could sleep. At length he reached a soft mossy bank under a tree, and was just about to stretch himself out on it, when a fearful roar made him start and tremble all over. In another moment something passed swiftly through the air and a lion stood before him.

"What are you doing here?" asked the lion, his eyes glaring fiercely at the boy.

"I am flying from the mermaid," the prince answered, in a quaking voice.

"Give me some food then," said the lion, "it is past my supper time, and I am very hungry."

The boy was so thankful that the lion did not want to eat him, that he gladly picked up his knapsack which

"The mermaid asks for the king's child."

lay on the ground, and held out some bread and a flask of wine.

"I feel better now," said the lion when he had done, "so now I shall go to sleep on this nice soft moss, and if you like you can lie down beside me." So the boy and the lion slept soundly side by side, till the sun rose.

"I must be off now," remarked the lion, shaking the boy as he spoke; "but cut off the tip of my ear, and keep it carefully, and if you are in any danger just wish yourself a lion and you will become one on the spot. One good turn deserves another, you know."

The prince thanked him for his kindness, and did as he was bid, and the two then bade each other farewell.

"I wonder how it feels to be a lion," thought the boy, after he had gone a little way; and he took out the tip of the ear from the breast of his jacket and wished with all his might. In an instant his head had swollen to several times its usual size, and his neck seemed very hot and heavy; and, somehow, his hands became paws, and his skin grew hairy and yellow. But what pleased him most was his long tail with a tuft at the end, which he lashed and switched proudly. "I like being a lion very much," he said to himself, and trotted gaily along the road.

After a while, however, he got tired of walking in this unaccustomed way–it made his back ache and his front paws felt sore. So he wished himself a boy again, and in the twinkling of an eye his tail disappeared and his head shrank, and the long thick mane became short and curly. Then he looked out for a sleeping place, and found some dry ferns, which he gathered and heaped up.

But before he had time to close his eyes there was a great noise in the trees nearby, as if a big heavy body was crashing through them. The boy rose and turned his head, and saw a huge black bear coming towards him.

"What are you doing here?" cried the bear.

"I am running away from the mermaid," answered the boy; but the bear took no interest in the mermaid, and only said: "I am hungry; give me something to eat."

The knapsack was lying on the ground among the fern, but the prince picked it up, and, unfastening the strap, took out his second flask of wine and another loaf of bread. "We will have supper together," he remarked politely; but the bear, who had never been taught manners, made no reply, and ate as fast as he could. When he had quite finished, he got up and stretched himself.

"You have got a comfortable-looking bed there," he observed. "I really think that, bad sleeper as I am; I might have a good night on it. I can manage to squeeze you in," he added; "you don't take up a great deal of room." The boy was rather indignant at the bear's cool way of talking; but as he was too tired to gather more fern, they lay down side by side, and never stirred till sunrise next morning.

"I must go now," said the bear, pulling the sleepy prince on to his feet; "but first you shall cut off the tip of my ear, and when you are in any danger just wish yourself a bear and you will become one. One good turn deserves another, you know." And the boy did as he was bid, and he and the bear bade each other farewell.

"I wonder how it feels to be a bear," thought he to himself when he had walked a little way; and he took out the tip from the breast of his coat and wished hard that he might become a bear. The next moment his body stretched out and thick black fur covered him all over. As before, his hands were changed into paws, but when he tried to switch his tail he found to his disgust that it would not go any distance. "Why it is hardly worth calling a tail!" said he. For the rest of the day he remained a bear and continued his journey, but as evening came on the bear-skin, which had been so useful when plunging through brambles in the forest, felt rather heavy, and he wished himself a boy again. He was too much exhausted to take the trouble of cutting any fern or seeking for moss, but just threw himself down under a tree, when exactly above his head he heard a great buzzing as a bumble-bee alighted on a honeysuckle branch. "What are you doing here?" asked the bee in a cross voice; "at your age you ought to be safe at home."

"I am running away from the mermaid," replied the boy; but the bee, like the lion and the bear, was one of those people who never listen to the answers to their questions, and only said: "I am hungry. Give me something to eat."

The boy took his last loaf and flask out of his knapsack and laid them on the ground, and they had supper together. "Well, now I am going to sleep," observed the bee when the last crumb was gone, "but as you are not very big I can make room for you beside me," and he curled up his wings, and tucked in his legs, and he and the prince both slept soundly till morning. Then the bee got up and carefully brushed every scrap of dust off his velvet coat and buzzed loudly in the boy's ear to waken him.

"Take a single hair from one of my wings," said he, "and if you are in danger just wish yourself a bee and you will become one. One good turn deserves another, so farewell, and thank you for your supper." And the bee departed after the boy had pulled out the hair and wrapped it carefully in a leaf.

"It must feel quite different to be a bee from what it does to be a lion or bear," thought the boy to himself when he had walked for an hour or two. "I dare say I should get on a great deal faster," so he pulled out his hair and wished himself a bee.

In a moment the strangest thing happened to him. All his limbs seemed to draw together, and his body to become very short and round; his head grew quite tiny, and instead of his white skin he was covered with the richest, softest velvet. Better than all, he had two lovely gauze wings which carried him the whole day without getting tired.

Late in the afternoon the boy fancied he saw a vast heap of stones a long way off, and he flew straight towards it. But when he reached the gates he saw that it was really a great town, so he wished himself back in his own shape and entered the city.

He found the palace doors wide open and went boldly into a sort of hall which was full of people, and where men and maids were gossiping together. He joined their talk and soon learned from them that the king had only one daughter who had such a hatred to men that she would never suffer one to enter her presence. Her father was in despair, and had had pictures painted of the handsomest princes of all the courts in the world, in the hope that she might fall in love with one of them; but it was no use; the princess would not even allow the pictures to be brought into her room.

"It is late," remarked one of the women at last; "I must go to my mistress." And, turning to one of the lackeys, she bade him find a bed for the youth.

The princess on the seashore.

"It is not necessary," answered the prince, "this bench is good enough for me. I am used to nothing better." And when the hall was empty he lay down for a few minutes. But as soon as everything was quiet in the palace he took out the hair and wished himself a bee, and in this shape he flew upstairs, past the guards, and through the keyhole into the princess's chamber. Then he turned himself into a man again.

At this dreadful sight the princess, who was broad awake, began to scream loudly. "A man! a man!" cried she; but when the guards rushed in there was only a bumble-bee buzzing about the room. They looked under the bed, and behind the curtains, and into the cupboards, then came to the conclusion that the princess had had a bad dream, and bowed themselves out. The door had scarcely closed on them than the bee disappeared, and a handsome youth stood in his place.

"I knew a man was hidden somewhere," cried the princess, and screamed more loudly than before. Her shrieks brought back the guards, but though they looked in all kinds of impossible places no man was to be seen, and so they told the princess.

"He was here a moment ago–I saw him with my own eyes," and the guards dared not contradict her, though they shook their heads and whispered to each other that the princess had gone mad on this subject, and saw a man in every table and chair. And they made up their minds that–let her scream as loudly as she might– they would take no notice.

Now the princess saw clearly what they were thinking, and that in future her guards would give her no help, and would perhaps, besides, tell some stories about her to the king, who would shut her up in a lonely tower and prevent her walking in the gardens among her birds and flowers. So when, for the third time, she beheld the prince standing before her, she did not scream but sat up in bed gazing at him in silent terror.

"Do not be afraid," he said, "I shall not hurt you"; and he began to praise her gardens, of which he had heard the servants speak, and the birds and flowers which she loved, till the princess's anger softened, and she answered him with gentle words. Indeed, they soon became so friendly that she vowed she would marry no one else, and confided to him that in three days her father would be off to the wars, leaving his sword in her room. If any man could find it and bring it to him he would receive her hand as a reward. At this point a cock crew, and the youth jumped up hastily saying: "Of course I shall ride with the king to the war, and if I do not return, take your violin every evening to the seashore and play on it, so that the very sea-kobolds who live at the bottom of the ocean may hear it and come to you."

Just as the princess had foretold, in three days the king set out for the war with a large following, and among them was the young prince, who had presented himself at court as a young noble in search of adventures. They had left the city many miles behind them, when the king suddenly discovered that he had forgotten his sword, and though all his attendants instantly offered theirs, he declared that he could fight with none but his own.

"The first man who brings it to me from my daughter's room," cried he, "shall not only have her to wife, but after my death shall reign in my stead."

At this the Red Knight, the young prince, and several more turned their horses to ride as fast as the wind back to the palace. But suddenly a better plan entered the prince's head, and, letting the others pass him, he took his precious parcel from his breast and wished himself a lion. Then on he bounded, uttering such dreadful roars that the horses were frightened and grew unmanageable, and he easily outstripped them, and soon reached the gates of the palace. Here he hastily changed himself into a bee, and flew straight into the princess's room, where he became a man again. She showed him where the sword hung concealed behind a curtain, and he took it down, saying as he did so: "Be sure not to forget what you have promised to do."

The princess made no reply, but smiled sweetly, and slipping a golden ring from her finger she broke it in two and held half out silently to the prince, while the other half she put in her own pocket. He kissed it, and ran down the stairs bearing the sword with him. Some way off he met the Red Knight and the rest, and the Red Knight at first tried to take the sword from him by force. But as the youth proved too strong for him, he gave it up, and resolved to wait for a better opportunity.

This soon came, for the day was hot and the prince was thirsty. Perceiving a little stream that ran into the sea, he turned aside, and, unbuckling the sword, flung himself on the ground for a long drink. Unluckily, the mermaid happened at that moment to be floating on the water not very far off, and knew he was the boy who had been given her before he was born. So she floated gently in to where he was lying, she seized him by the arm, and the waves closed over them both. Hardly had they disappeared, when the Red Knight stole cautiously up, and could hardly believe his eyes when he saw the king's sword on the bank. He wondered what had become of the youth, who an hour before had guarded his treasure so fiercely; but, after all, that was no affair of his! So, fastening the sword to his belt, he carried it to the king.

The war was soon over, and the king returned to his people, who welcomed him with shouts of joy. But when the princess from her window saw that her betrothed was not among the attendants riding behind her father, her heart sank, for she knew that some evil must have befallen him. and she feared the Red Knight. She had long ago learned how clever and how wicked he was, and something whispered to her that it was he who would gain the credit of having carried back the sword, and would claim her as his bride, though he had never even entered her chamber. And she could do nothing; for although the king loved her, he never let her stand in the way of his plans.

The poor princess was only too right, and everything came to pass exactly as she had foreseen it. The king told her that the Red Knight had won her fairly, and that the wedding would take place next day, and there would be a great feast after it.

In those days feasts were much longer and more splendid than they are now; and it was growing dark when the princess, tired out with all she had gone through, stole up to her own room for a little quiet. But the moon was shining so brightly over the sea that it seemed to draw her towards it, and taking her violin under her arm, she crept down to the shore.

"Listen! listen! said the mermaid to the prince, who was lying stretched on a bed of seaweeds at the bottom of the sea. "Listen! that is your old love playing, for mermaids know everything that happens upon earth."

"I hear nothing," answered the youth, who did not look happy. "Take me up higher, where the sounds can reach me."

So the mermaid took him on her shoulders and bore him up midway to the surface. "Can you hear now?" she asked.

"No," answered the prince, "I hear nothing but the water rushing; I must go higher still."

Then the mermaid carried him to the very top. "You must surely be able to hear now?" said she.

"Nothing but the water," repeated the youth. So she took him right to the land.

"At any rate you can hear now?" she said again.

"The water is still rushing in my ears," answered he; " but wait a little, that will soon pass off." And as he spoke he put his hand into his breast, and seizing the hair wished himself a bee, and flew straight into the pocket of the princess. The mermaid looked in vain for him, and coated all night upon the sea; but he never came back, and never more did he gladden her eyes. But the princess felt that something strange was about her, though she knew not what, and returned quickly to the palace, where the young man at once resumed his own shape. Oh, what joy filled her heart at the sight of him! But there was no time to be lost, and she led him right into the hall, where the king and his nobles were still sitting at the feast. "Here is a man who boasts that he can do wonderful tricks," said she, "better even than the Red Knight's! That cannot be true, of course, but it might be well to give this impostor a lesson. He pretends, for instance, that he can turn himself into a lion; but that I do not believe. I know that you have studied the art of magic," she went on, turning to the Red Knight, "so suppose you just show him how it is done, and bring shame upon him."

Now the Red Knight had never opened a book of magic in his life; but he was accustomed to think that he could do everything better than other people without any teaching at all. So he turned and twisted himself about, and bellowed and made faces; but he did not become a lion for all that.

"Well, perhaps it is very difficult to change into a lion. Make yourself a bear," said the princess. But the Red Knight found it no easier to become a bear than a lion.

"Try a bee," suggested she. "I have always read that anyone who can do magic at all can do that." And the old knight buzzed and hummed, but he remained a man and not a bee.

"Now it is your turn," said the princess to the youth. "Let us see if you can change yourself into a lion." And in a moment such a fierce creature stood before them, that all the guests rushed out of the hall, treading each other underfoot in their fright. The lion sprang at the Red Knight, and would have torn him in pieces had not the princess held him back, and bidden him to change himself into a man again. And in a second a man took the place of the lion.

"Now become a bear," said she; and a bear advanced panting and stretching out his arms to the Red Knight, who shrank behind the princess.

By this time some of the guests had regained their courage, and returned as far as the door, thinking that if it was safe for the princess perhaps it was safe for them. The king, who was braver than they, and felt it needful to set them a good example besides, had never left his seat, and when at a new command of the princess the bear once more turned into a man, he was silent from astonishment, and a suspicion of the truth began to dawn on him. "Was it he who fetched the sword?" asked the king.

"Yes, it was," answered the princess; and she told him the whole story, and how she had broken her gold ring and given him half of it. And the prince took out his half of the ring, and the princess took out hers, and they fitted exactly. Next day the Red Knight was hanged, as he richly deserved, and there was a new marriage feast for the prince and princess.

NATIVE AMERICAN

Ne Hwas, the Mermaid

CHARLES G. LELAND

ILLUSTRATIONS EDUARD BUK ULREICH

Editor's note: *This is a Passamaquoddy legend. The term "Indian" has been taken from the original 1880's text account of the story.*

A long time ago there was an Indian, with his wife and two daughters. They lived by a great lake, or the sea, and the mother told her girls never to go into the water there, for that, if they did, something would happen to them.

They, however, deceived her repeatedly. When swimming is prohibited it becomes delightful. The shore of this lake sands away out or slopes to an island. One day they went to it, leaving their clothes on the beach. The parents missed them.

The father went to seek them. He saw them swimming far out, and called to them. The girls swam up to the sand, but could get no further. Their father asked them why they could not. They cried that they had grown to be so heavy that it was impossible. They were all slimy; they grew to be snakes from below the waist. After sinking a few times in this strange slime they became very handsome, with long black hair and large, bright black eyes, with silver bands on their neck and arms. When their father went to get their clothes, they began to sing in the most exquisite tones:

"Leave them there!
Do not touch them!
Leave them there!"

Hearing this, their mother began to weep, but the girls kept on:

"It is all our own fault,
But do not blame us;
"It will be none the worse for you.
When you go in your canoe,
Then you need not paddle;
We shall carry it along!"

And so it was: when their parents went in the canoe, the girls carried it safely on everywhere. One day some Indians saw the girls clothes on the beach, and so looked out for the wearers. They found them in the water, and pursued them, and tried to capture them, but they were so slimy that it was impossible to take them, till one, catching hold of a mermaid by her long black hair, cut it off.

Then the girl began to rock the canoe, and threatened to upset it unless her hair was given to her again. The fellow who had played the trick at first refused, but as the mermaids, or snake-maids, promised that they should all be drowned unless this was done, the locks were restored. And the next day they were heard singing and were seen, and on her who had lost her hair it was all growing as long as ever.

The Mermaid

FRIEDRICH REINHOLD KREUTZWALD
ILLUSTRATIONS CHARLES MURRAY PADDA

I n the happy days of old, better men lived on earth than now, and the Heavenly Father revealed many wonders to them which are now quite concealed, or but rarely manifested to a child of fortune. It is true that the birds sing and the beasts converse as of old, but unhappily we no longer comprehend their speech, and what they say brings us neither profit nor wisdom.

In old days a fair mermaid dwelt on the shores of the province of Lääne. She often appeared to the people, and my grandfather's father, who was reared in the neighbourhood, sometimes saw her sitting on a rock, but the little fellow did not venture to approach her. The maiden appeared in various forms, sometimes as a foal or a calf, and sometimes under the form of some other animal. In the evening she often came among the children, and let them play with her, until some little boy mounted her back, when she would vanish as suddenly as if she had sunk into the ground.

At that time old people said that in former days the maiden was to be seen on the borders of the sea almost every fine evening in the summer, sitting on a rock, and combing her long fair hair with a golden comb, and she sang such beautiful songs that it melted the hearts of her listeners. But she could not endure the gaze of men, and vanished from their sight or fled into the sea, where she rocked on the waves like a swan. We will now relate the cause of her flying from men, and no longer meeting them with her former confidence.

In old times, long before the invasion of the Swedes, a rich farmer lived on the coast of Lääne with his wife and four sons. They obtained their food more from the sea than from the land, for fishing was a very productive industry in their days. The youngest son was very different from his brothers, even from a child. He avoided the companionship of men, and wandered about on the sea-shore and in the forest. He talked much to himself and to the birds, or to the winds and waves, but when he was in the company of others he hardly opened his mouth, but stood like one dreaming.

When the storms raged over the sea in autumn, and the waves swelled up as high as a house and broke foaming on the beach, the boy could not contain himself in the house, but ran like one possessed, and often half-naked, to the shore. Neither wind nor weather harmed his robust body. He sprang into his boat, seized the oars, and drove like a wild goose over the crest of the raging billows far out to sea, without incurring any harm by his rashness. In the morning, when the storm had spent its fury, he was found sound asleep on the beach. If he was sent anywhere on an errand, to herd cattle in summer, or to do any other easy employment, he gave his parents only trouble. He lay down under the shadow of a bush without minding the animals, and they strayed away or trampled down the meadows and cornfields, and his brothers had often to work for hours before they could find the lost animals. The father often let the boy feel the rod severely enough, but it had no more effect than water poured on the back of a goose. When the boy grew up into a youth, he did not mend his ways. No work prospered in his negligent hands; he hacked and broke the tools, wearied out the draught cattle, and yet never did anything right.

His father sent him to neighbouring farmers to work, hoping that a stranger's whip might improve the sloven, but whoever had the fellow for one week on trial sent him back again on the next. His parents rated him for a sluggard, and his brothers dubbed him "Sleepy Tony." This soon became his nickname with everybody, though he had been christened Jüri. Sleepy Tony brought no one any good, but was only a nuisance to his parents and relatives, so that they would gladly have given a sum of money if anybody would have rid them of the lazy fellow. As nobody would put up with him any longer, his father engaged him as servant to a foreign captain, because he could not run away at sea, and because he had always been so fond of the water from a child. However, after a few weeks, nobody knows how, he escaped from the ship, and again set his lazy feet on his native soil. But he was ashamed to enter his father's house, where he could not expect to meet with a friendly reception, so he wandered about from one place to another, and sought to get his living as he could, without working. He was a strong handsome fellow, and could talk very agreeably if he liked, although he had never been accustomed to talk much in his father's house. He was now obliged to use his handsome appearance and fine tongue to ingratiate himself with the women and girls.

One fine summer evening after sunset it happened that he was wandering alone on the beach when the clear song of the mermaid reached his ears. Sleepy Tony thought to himself, "She is a woman, at any rate, and won't do me any harm." He did not hesitate to approach nearer, to take a view of the beautiful bird. He climbed the highest hill, and saw the mermaid some distance off, sitting on a rock, combing her hair with a golden comb, and singing a ravishing song. The youth would have wished for more ears to listen to her song, which pierced his heart like a flame, but when he drew nearer he saw that he would have needed just as many eyes to take in the beauty of the maiden. The mermaid must have seen him coming, but she did not fly from him, as she was always wont to do when men approached. Sleepy Tony advanced to within ten paces of her, and then stopped, undecided whether to go nearer. And oh, wonderful! the mermaid rose from the stone and came to meet him with a friendly air.

She gave him her hand in greeting, and said, "I have expected you for many days, for a fateful dream warned me of your arrival. You have neither house nor home among those of your own race. Why should you be dependent upon strangers when your parents refuse to receive you into their house? I have known you from a child, and better than men have known you, for I have often watched over and protected you when your rashness would otherwise have destroyed you. I have often guarded the rocking boat with my hands, when it would otherwise have sunk in the depths. Come with me, and you shall enjoy every happiness which your heart can desire, and you shall want for nothing. I will watch over and protect you as the apple of my eye, so that neither wind nor rain nor frost shall touch you."

Sleepy Tony stood for a time uncertain what to answer, though every word of the maiden was like a flaming arrow in his heart. At last he stammered out an inquiry as to whether her home was very far away. "We can reach it with the speed of the wind, if you have confidence in me," answered the mermaid. Then Sleepy Tony remembered many sayings which he had heard about the mermaid, and his heart failed him, and he asked for three days to make up his mind.

"I will agree to your wish," said the mermaid, "but lest you should again be doubtful, I will put my gold ring on your finger before we part, that you may not forget to return. When we are better acquainted, this pledge may serve as an engagement ring." She then drew off the ring, placed it on the youth's little finger, and vanished as if she had melted into air. Sleepy Tony stood staring with wide-open eyes, and would have supposed it was all a dream, if the sparkling ring on his finger had not been proof to the contrary. But the ring seemed like a strange spirit, which left him no peace or rest anywhere. He wandered aimlessly about the shore all night, and always returned to the rock on which the maiden had been sitting; but the stone was cold and vacant.

In the morning he lay down for a short time, but uneasy dreams disturbed his sleep. When he awoke, he felt neither hunger nor thirst, and all his thoughts were directed towards the evening, when he hoped to see the mermaid again. The day waned at last, and evening approached, the wind sank, the birds in the alder-bushes left off singing and tucked their tired heads under their wings, but that evening he saw the mermaid nowhere.

He wept bitter tears of sorrow and trouble, and reflected bitterly on his folly in having hesitated to seize the good fortune offered to him the evening before, when a cleverer fellow would have grasped at it with both hands. But regret and complaint were useless now. The night and the day which followed were equally painful to him, and his trouble weighed upon him so much that he never felt hunger. Towards sunset he sat down with an aching heart on the rock where the mermaid had sat two evenings ago. He began to weep bitterly, and exclaimed, sobbing, "If she does not come back to me, I will live no longer, but either die of hunger on this rock, or cast myself headlong into the waves, and end my miserable life in the depths of the sea."

I know not how long he sat thus on the rock in his distress, but at last he felt a soft warm hand laid upon his forehead. When he looked up, he saw the maiden before him, and she said tenderly, "I have seen your bitter suffering and heard your longing sighs, and could not withdraw myself longer, though the time does not expire till to-morrow night."

"Forgive me, forgive me, dear maiden," stammered Sleepy Tony. "Forgive me; I was a mad fool not to accept the proffered happiness. The devil only knows what folly came into my head two nights ago. Carry me whither you please. I will oppose you no longer, and would joyfully give up my very life for your sake."

The mermaid answered smiling, "I do not desire your death, but I will take you living as my dear companion." She took the youth by the hand, led him a few paces nearer to the sea, and bound a silk handkerchief over his eyes. Immediately Sleepy Tony felt himself embraced by two strong arms, which raised him up as if in flight, and then plunged headlong into the sea. The moment the cold water touched his body, he lost all consciousness, and knew nothing more of what was happening around him; nor was he afterwards able to tell how long this insensibility lasted. When he awoke, he was to experience something stranger still.

He found himself lying on soft cushions in a silken bed, which stood in a beautiful chamber, with walls of glass covered on the inside with curtains of red satin, lest the glaring light should wake the sleeper. Some time passed before he could make out whether he was still alive, or whether he was in some unknown region of the dead. He rocked his limbs to and fro, took the end of his nose between his fingers, and behold, he was quite unchanged. He was dressed in a white shirt, and handsome clothes lay in a chair in front of his bed. After lying in bed for some time, and feeling himself all over to make sure that he was really alive, he got up and dressed himself.

Presently he coughed, when two maids entered, who greeted him as "his lordship," and wished to know what he would like for breakfast. One laid the table, and the other went to prepare the food. In a short time the table was loaded with dishes of pork, sausage, black puddings, and honey, with jugs of beer and mead, just the same as at a grand wedding-feast. Sleepy Tony, who had eaten nothing for several days before, now set to work in earnest, and ate his fill, after which he laid down on the bed to digest it. When he got up again, the waiting-maids came back, and invited his lordship to take a walk in the garden while her ladyship was dressing. He heard himself called "your lordship" so often, that he already began to feel himself such in reality, and forgot his former station.

In the garden he met with beauty and elegance at every step; gold and silver apples glittered among the green leaves, and even the fir and pine cones were of gold, while birds of golden plumage hopped among the twigs and branches. Two maids came from behind a bush, who were commissioned to show his lordship round the garden, and to point out all its beauties. They went farther, and reached the edge of a pond where silver-feathered geese and swans were swimming. A rosy flush as of dawn filled all the sky, but the sun was not visible. The bushes were covered with flowers which exhaled a delicious odour, and bees as large as hornets flew among the flowers. All the flowers and shrubs which our friend beheld here were far more beautiful than he had ever seen before. Presently two elegantly dressed girls appeared, who invited his lordship to meet her ladyship, who was expecting him. But first they threw a blue silken shawl over his shoulders. Who would have recognised the former Sleepy Tony in such a guise?

In a beautiful hall, as large as a church, and built of glass like the bedroom, sat twelve fair maidens on silver chairs. Against the wall behind them was a dais on which two golden thrones were placed. On one throne sat the august queen, and the other was unoccupied. When Sleepy Tony crossed the threshold, all the maidens rose from their seats and saluted him respectfully, and did not sit down again until desired to do so. The lady herself remained seated, bent her head to the youth in salutation, and signed with her finger, upon which Sleepy Tony's attendants took him between them, and conducted him to their mistress. The youth advanced with faltering steps, and did not venture to lift his eyes, for he was dazzled with all the unaccustomed splendour and magnificence. He was shown to his place on the golden throne next to the lady, and she said, "This young man is my beloved bridegroom, to whom I have plighted myself and whom I have accepted as my consort. You must show him every respect, and obey him as you obey me. Whenever I leave the house, you must amuse him and look after him and guard him as the apple of my eye. You will be severely punished if you neglect to carry out my orders exactly."

Sleepy Tony looked round him like one dazed, for he did not know what to make of the adventures of the night, which were more wonderful than wonder itself. He continually turned the question over in his mind as to whether he was awake or dreaming. The lady noticed his confusion, and rose from her throne, took him by the hand, and led him from one room to another, all of which were untenanted. At last they arrived at the twelfth chamber, which was rather smaller, but handsomer than the others. Here the lady took her crown from her bead, cast aside the gold-embroidered mantle, and when Sleepy Tony ventured to raise his eyes, he recognised that it was the mermaid at his side, and no strange lady. Oh, how quickly his courage rose and his hopes revived!

He cried out joyfully, "O dear mermaid!" — but the maiden laid her hand on his mouth, and spoke very earnestly, "If you have any regard for your own happiness or for mine, never call me by that name, which has only been given to me in mockery. I am one of the daughters of the Water-Mother. There are many sisters of us, but we all live apart, each in her own place, in the sea, or in lakes and rivers, and we only see each other occasionally by some fortunate chance."

She then explained to him that she had hitherto remained unmarried, but now that she was an established ruler, she must assume the dignity of a royal matron. Sleepy Tony was so bewildered with this unimagined good fortune that he did not know how to express his happiness. His tongue seemed paralysed, and he could not manage to say more than Yes or No. But while he was enjoying a capital dinner and delicious beverages, his tongue was loosened, and he was not only able to talk as well as before, but to indulge in many pleasant jests.

This agreeable life was continued on the next and on the third day, and Sleepy Tony thought he had been exalted to heaven in his living body. But before retiring to rest the mermaid said to him, "Tomorrow will be

Thursday, and every week I am bound by a vow to fast, and to remain apart from every one. You cannot see me at all on Thursdays until the cock has crowed thrice in the evening. My attendants will sing to you to pass the time away, and will see that you want for nothing."

Next morning Sleepy Tony could not find his consort anywhere. He remembered what she had told him the evening before, that he must pass this and all future Thursdays without her. The waiting-maids exerted themselves to amuse him in every possible manner; they sang, played, and performed elegant dances, and then set before him such food and drink that no prince by birthright could have enjoyed better, and the day passed quicker than he had expected. After supper he laid himself to rest, and when the cock had crowed three times, the fair one returned to him. The same thing happened on every following Thursday. He often implored his beloved to allow him to fast with her on Thursdays, but all to no purpose. He troubled his consort again on a Wednesday with this request, and allowed her no rest; but the mermaid said, with tears in her eyes, "Take my life, if you please; I would lay it down cheerfully; but I cannot and dare not yield to your wish to take you with me on my fast-days."

A year or more might have passed in this manner, when doubts arose in the mind of Sleepy Tony, which became always more tormenting, and allowed him no peace. His food became distasteful to him and his sleep refreshed him not. He feared lest the mermaid might have some other lover in secret besides himself, in whose arms she passed every Thursday, while he was obliged to pass his time with the waiting-maids. He had long ago discovered the room in which the mermaid hid herself on Thursdays, but how did that help him?

The door was always locked, and the windows were so closely hung with double curtains on the inside that there was not an opening left as large as a needle's eye through which a sunbeam, much less a human eye, could penetrate. But the more impossible it seemed to penetrate this secret, the more eager grew his longing to get to the very bottom of it. Although he never breathed a word of the weight upon his mind to the mermaid, she could see from his altered manner that all was not as it should be. Again and again she implored him with tears in her eyes not to torment both himself and her with evil thoughts. "I am free from every fault against you," she declared, "and I have no secret love nor any other sin against you on my conscience. But your false suspicion makes us both miserable, and will destroy the peace of our hearts. I would gladly give up every moment of my life to you if you wished it, but I cannot allow you to come near me on my fast-days. It cannot be, for it would put an end to our love and happiness forever. We are able to live quietly and happily together for six days in the week, and how should the separation of one day be so heavy that you cannot bear it?"

She talked in this sensible way for six days, but when the following Thursday came, and the mermaid did not show herself, Sleepy Tony lost his wits, and behaved as if he was half-mad. He knew no peace, and at last one Thursday he refused to have any one with him. He ordered the waiting-maids to bring him his food and drink, and then to leave him directly, so that he remained alone like a spectre.

This great alteration in his conduct astonished everybody, and when the mermaid heard of the matter, she almost wept her eyes out of her head, though she only gave way to her grief when no one was present. Sleepy Tony hoped that when he was alone he might have a better opportunity of inspecting the secret fasting chamber, and perhaps he might find some crack through which he could spy upon what was going on. The more he tormented himself, the more depressed became the mermaid, and although she still maintained a cheerful countenance, her friendliness no longer came from the heart as before.

Some weeks passed by, and matters remained at a standstill, neither worse nor better, when one Thursday Sleepy Tony found a small space near the window where the curtains had slightly shifted, so that he could look into the chamber. The secret chamber had no floor, but looked like a great square tank, filled with water many feet deep. Herein swam his much-loved mermaid. From her head to her middle she was a beautiful woman, but from the navel downwards she was wholly a fish, covered with scales and provided with fins. Sometimes she threshed the water with her broad fish's tail and it dashed high up.

The spy shrunk back confounded and made his way home very sorrowfully. What would he not have given to have blotted the sight from his memory! He thought of one thing and another, but could not decide on what to do.

In the evening the cock crowed three times as usual, but the mermaid did not come back to him. He lay awake all night, but the fair one never came. She did not return till morning, when she was clad in black mourning garments and her face was covered with a thin silk handkerchief. Then she said, weeping, "O thou unhappy one! to have brought our happy life to an end by thy folly! Thou seest me today for the last time, and must return to thy former condition, and this thou hast brought upon thyself. Farewell, for the last time."

There was a sudden crash and a tremendous noise, as if the floor was giving way beneath his feet, and Sleepy Tony was hurled down stunned, and could not perceive what was happening to himself or about him.

No one knows how long afterwards it may have been when he recovered from his swoon, and found himself on the sea-shore close to the rock on which the fair mermaid had sat when she entered into the bond of friendship with him. Instead of the magnificent robes which be had worn every day in the dwelling of the mermaid, he found himself dressed in his old clothes, which were now much older and more ragged than he could possibly have supposed. Our friend's happy days were over, and no remorse, however bitter, could bring them back.

He walked on till he reached the first houses of his village. They were standing in the same places, but yet looked different. But what appeared to him much more wonderful when he looked round, was that the people were all strangers, and he did not meet a single face which he knew.

The people all looked strangely at him, too, as though he was a monster. Sleepy Tony went on to the farm of his parents, but here too he encountered only strangers, who knew him not, and whom he did not know. He asked in amazement for his father and brothers, but no one could tell him anything about them. At length an infirm old man came up, leaning on a stick, and said, "Peasant, the farmer whom you ask after has been sleeping in the ground for more than thirty years, and his sons must be dead too. How comes it, my good old man, that you ask after people who have been so long forgotten?"

The words "old man" took Sleepy Tony so much aback that he was unable to ask another question. He felt his limbs trembling, turned his back on the strange people, and went out at the gate. The expression "old man" left him no peace; it fell upon him with a crushing weight, and his feet refused him their office.

He hurried to the nearest spring and gazed in the water. The pale sunken cheeks, the hollow eyes, the long grey beard and grey hair, confirmed what he had heard. This worn-out, withered form no longer bore the slightest resemblance to the youth whom the mermaid had chosen as her consort. Now he fully realised his misery for the first time, and knew that the few years that he appeared to have been absent had comprised the greater part of his life, for he had entered the mermaid's house as a vigorous youth, and had returned as a spectre-like old man. There he had felt nothing of the course of time or of the wasting of his body, and he could not comprehend how the burden of old age had fallen upon him so suddenly, like the passing of a bird's wing. What could he do now, when he was a grey stranger among strangers?

He wandered about on the beach for a few days, from one farm to another, and good people gave him a piece of bread out of charity. He chanced to meet with a friendly young fellow, to whom he related all the adventures of his life, but the same night he disappeared. A few days afterwards the waves cast up his body on the shore. It is not known whether he threw himself into the sea, or was drowned by accident.

After this the behaviour of the mermaid towards mankind entirely changed. She sometimes appears to children only, most often in another form, but she does not permit grown-up people to approach her, but shuns them like fire.

NORSE

The Girl and the Fish

GEORGE WEBBE DASENT
ILLUSTRATIONS ARTHUR RACKHAM

T here was once a girl who used to go to the river to fetch water, but when she went she was never in a hurry to come back, but stayed so long, that they made up their minds to watch her. So one day they followed her to the river, and found when she got there she said something (the reciter forgets the words), and a fish came up and talked to her; and she did not like to leave it, for it was her sweetheart.

So they went next day to the river to see if the fish would come up, for they remembered what the girl said, and used the same words. Then up came the fish immediately, and they caught it, and took it home, and cooked it for dinner, and a part they set by, and gave it to the girl when she came in. Whilst she was eating, a voice said, "Do you know what you are eating? I am he you have so often talked with. If you look in the pig's tub you will see my heart."

Then the voice told her to take the heart, and wrap it up in a handkerchief, and carry it to the river. When she got to the river she would see three stones in the water; she was to stand on the middle stone and dip the handkerchief three times into the water. All this she did, and then she sank suddenly, and was carried down to a beautiful place, where she found her lover changed from a fish into his proper form, and there she lived happily with him forever. And this is the reason why there are mermaids in the water.

The Mermaid's Child

Abbie Farwell Brown

Illustrations Amelia Bauerle (Bowerley)

I n the rocks on the seashore, left bare by the tide, one often finds tiny pools of water fringed with seaweed and padded with curious moss. These are the cradles which the Mermaids have trimmed prettily for the sea-babies, and where they leave the little ones when they have to go away on other business, as Mermaids do. But one never spies the sea-children in their cradles, for they are taught to tumble out and slip away into the sea if a human step should approach. You see, the fishes have told the Mer-folk cruel tales of the Land-people with their nets and hooks and lines.

In the softest, prettiest little cradle of all a Sea-child lay one afternoon crying to himself. He cried because he was lonesome. His mother did not love him as a baby's mother should; for she was the silliest and the vainest of all the Mermaids. Her best friend was her looking-glass of polished pearl, and her only care was to remain young and girlish. Indeed, she bore her thousand-odd years well, even for a Mermaid. She liked the Sea-baby well enough, but she was ashamed to have him follow her about as he loved to do, because she imagined it made her seem old to be called "Mer-mother" by his lisping lips. She never had time to caress or play with him; and finally she forbade him ever to speak to her unless she spoke first. Sometimes she seemed to forget him altogether, as she left him to take care of himself, while she sat on the rocks combing her long green hair, or playing with the giddy Mermen in the caves below the sea.

So while the other sea-people sported or slept and were happy, her poor little Sea-child lay and cried in the green pool where the sea-anemones tickled his cheek with their soft fingers, seeking to make him laugh, and the sea-fringe curled about the scaly little tail which, like a fish, he had in place of legs. On this particular afternoon he was particularly lonesome.

"Ahoo!" he sobbed. "I am so unhappy! Ahoo! I want some one to love me very much!"

Now a kind old Stork was sitting on a rock above the baby's head, preening his feathers in a looking-glass pool. He heard the Sea-child's words, and he spoke in his kind, gruff voice.

"What is the matter, little one?" he asked.

At first the Sea-child was surprised to be addressed by a land bird. But he soon saw that this creature was friendly, and told him all his trouble, as babies do. "Tut tut!" said the Stork, frowning. "Your Mer-mother needs a lesson sadly."

"What is a lesson?" lisped the Sea-child.

But the Stork was busy thinking and did not reply at once. "How would you like a change?" he asked after a time.

"What is a change?" asked the baby, for he was very young and ignorant.

"You shall see," answered the Stork, "if you will take my advice; for I am your friend. Now listen. When next you hear a step upon the rocks do not stir from your cradle, but wait and see what will happen." Without another word the Stork flapped away, leaving the baby to stare up at the blue sky with the tears still wet upon his cheeks, wondering what the Stork could have meant.

"I will not stir," he said to himself. "Whatever happens I will wait and see."

It was the Stork's business to bring babies to the homes where babies were needed; and sometimes it was very hard to find babies enough. Even now he knew of a house upon the hill where a boy was longing for a little brother to play with. Every night Gil mentioned the matter in his prayers; every night he begged the Stork to bring him a playmate. But though the Stork had hunted far and wide through all the land he could not find a human baby to spare for the cottage on the hill. Now he had a happy idea.

With his long legs dangling he flew swiftly up towards the hill; and halfway there he met the boy wandering about sulkily all alone. The Stork had never before spoken to this boy, because he well knew what Gil wanted, and he hated to be teased for what he could not give. So, though he had listened sadly to the boy's prayers, by day he had kept carefully out of sight. But now he came close overhead, and settling down stood upon one leg directly in Gil's path.

"Good-afternoon," he said. "I think I have heard you say that you wanted a little brother."

Gil was surprised to have a Stork address him like this, but he was still more pleased at the happy word. "I do! Oh, I do indeed!" he cried.

"Would you make a good brother to him?" asked the Stork.

"Oh yes!" answered the boy eagerly. "A very good brother I should be."

"H'm," said the Stork. "One never can tell about these boys. I think you are selfish and jealous. But a little brother may be a good thing for you. In any case, there is little for him to lose. Will you be so good as to come with me?"

Without another word the Stork flew up and away toward the beach, leaving Gil staring. This certainly was a most extraordinary bird! But Gil soon decided to follow him and see what would happen, for who could tell what the Stork's mysterious words might mean?

Presently, lying in his little cradle, the Sea-child heard the sound of feet scrambling up the rocks,—the sound he had been taught to fear more than anything in the world. It was his first thought to flop out of the cradle, over into the sea below; and he half turned to do so. But in a moment he remembered the Stork's last words, and although he was trembling with fear he remained where he was.

Soon over the top of the rock peered the face of the boy, Gil of the hill cottage, looking straight down into the pool where the Sea-baby lay snugly on the seaweed.

"Oh!" cried the boy, with round black eyes fixed upon the baby's round blue ones. "Oh!" cried the Sea-child. And it would be hard to say which of the two was more astonished. For to a Sea-child the sight of clothed, two-legged land-boy is quite as strange as a naked little fish-tailed infant is to a human. But after the first look neither felt afraid, in spite of the terrible tales which each had heard of the other's kind. They stared wistfully at each other, not knowing what to do next, until the Stork came forward and spoke wise words.

"You, land-boy Gil," he said, "you want a little brother, do you not?" Gil nodded. "And you, Sea-child, want someone to love you? I think I can manage to please you both. But first you must kiss each other."

Gil hesitated. He was a big boy of five or six, too old for kissing. Moreover the Sea-child looked cold and wet and somewhat fishy. But already the red lips of the little fellow were pouted into a round O, and the sad blue eyes were looking up at him so pleadingly that Gil bent low over the watery cradle. Then two little soft arms went about his neck, and Gil felt the heart of the Sea-child thump happily against his own.

"Very good," said the Stork approvingly.

The Sea-child could not stand, on account of having no feet, but he lay in his pool holding Gil's hand.

"Now the change is coming," went on the Stork, and as he spoke the baby began to fall asleep. "In twelve hours," he said to Gil, "he will become a tiny human child, and I shall carry him to the house on the hill, where he will find a loving family awaiting him. Look! Already he is losing the uniform of the sea," and he pointed at the Sea-child's fishy tail. Sure enough, the scales were falling away one by one, and already the shape of two little chubby legs could be seen under the skin, which was shrinking as a tadpole's does before he becomes a frog. "When this tail is wholly gone," declared the Stork, "he will forget what we have said to-night. He will forget his sea-home and the caves of the Mer-people. He will forget that he was once a Sea-child; and no one will ever remind him. For only you, Gil, and I shall know the secret."

"And I shall never tell," declared Gil.

"No, surely you will never tell," answered the Stork gravely, "for if you tell that will be the end of all. You will lose the little brother, and you will be sorry all the rest of your life. Do not forget, Gil. Do not forget."

"I shall not forget," said Gil.

Again they looked at the Sea-child, and he had fallen sound asleep, still holding Gil's hand. Now there was scarcely anything of the fish left about his little pink body; he was growing younger and younger, smaller and smaller.

"You must go home now, Gil," said the Stork. "Go home and go to bed. And tomorrow when you wake there will be a little brother in the house, and you ought to be a very good boy because you have your wish."

Gil gently loosened the Sea-child's hand and ran home as the Stork bade him, but said no word of all this to anyone.

Now early in the morning the Stork came to the house on the hill, bringing a rosy little new baby which he laid on the bed beside Gil's mother, and then flew away. What a hullabaloo there was then, to be sure! What a welcome for the little stranger! Gil was not the only one who had longed for a new baby in the house, and this was the prettiest little fellow ever seen. Loudest of all cheered Gil when he saw the present which the Stork had brought. "Hurrah for my little new brother!" he cried. "Now I shall have someone to play with." That was Gil's chief thought: now he would have someone to play with.

They called the baby's name Jan. And from the first little Jan was very happy in his new home. He was happy all day in his mother's arms; happy when his foster-father came home at night and tossed him high to the ceiling; happiest of all when Gil held him close and begged him to hurry and grow up, so that they could play together.

Little Jan did hurry to grow up, as fast as health and strength and happiness could make a baby grow. He grew bigger and bigger, handsomer and handsomer, the finest baby in the village, and his family loved him dearly. Every day he became more of a playmate for Gil, whom he admired more than anyone in the world. Gil petted and teased the little fellow, who, as soon as he could walk, began to follow him about like a faithful dog. Grand times the brothers had together then. They dug in the sand on the seashore, and scrambled about the cliffs. They rowed out in the harbor boats with hooks and lines, and played at being fishermen like their father, who sailed away early and came home late. They grew bigger and sturdier and handsomer, and their parents were very proud of them both, the finest lads in all the country round.

The years went by, and during all this time Jan never dreamed the truth which only Gil and the Stork knew about the bargain made at the sea-pool cradle. To Jan, indeed, the sea was full of strange thoughts which were not memories but were like them. He loved to look and listen alone upon the water, or in the water, or by the water. Gil often[80] caught him staring down

161

into the blue waves, and when he raised his head there would be a puzzled look in the little fellow's blue eyes, as though he were trying to solve a riddle. Then Gil would laugh; whereat the wrinkle would smooth itself from Jan's forehead, and a smile would come about his mouth. He would throw his arm about his brother's shoulder, saying, —

"What strange thing is it, brother that the old sea does to me? I think sometimes that I am bewitched." But Gil would only laugh again, thinking his own thoughts. It gave him a pleasant important feeling to know that he was the keeper of Jan's secret.

Meantime what had become of the Sea-baby's forgotten mother? What was the pretty Mermaid doing in her home under the waves? She was learning the lesson which the Stork had meant to teach.

At first she had not greatly missed the Sea-baby, having other things to interest her in the lovely world where she lived. But as the sea-days went by she began to find the[81] grotto which had been their pretty home a very lonely place indeed. She missed the little fellow playing with the shells and starfish on the floor of shining sand. She longed to see him teasing the crabs in the crevices of the rocks, or tickling the sea-anemones to make them draw in their waving fingers. She missed the round blue eyes which used to look at her so admiringly, and the little hands which had once wearied her with their caresses. She even missed the mischievous tricks which the baby sometimes used to play upon his mother, and she would have been glad once more to see him running away with her pearly mirror, or with the golden comb with which she combed her long green hair.

As she watched the other sea-children playing merrily with the fishes the lonely Mermaid grew very sad, for she knew that her own baby had been the prettiest of them all, and she wondered how she could ever have been ashamed of him. The other mothers were proud of their darlings, and now they scorned her because she had no little one to hold her mirror when she made her toilet, or to run her errands when she was busy at play. But the poor Mermaid was too sad to play nowadays. She no longer took any pleasure in the happy life which the Mer-folk lived beneath the waves. She wandered instead here and there, up and down the sea, calling, calling for her lost baby. The sound of her sobbing came from the sea at morning, noon, and night.

She did not know her child's fate, but she feared that he had been captured by the dreadful Men-folk, who, so her people said, were ever seeking to snare the sea-creatures in their wicked nets. Day after day the unhappy Mermaid swam along the shore trying to see the places where the Men-folk dwelt, hoping that she might catch a glimpse of her lost darling. But that good hap never befell her. Indeed, even if she had seen Jan, she would not have known her baby in the sturdy boy dressed all in blue, like the other fisher-lads. Nor would Jan have known his mother in this beautiful creature of the sea. For he had quite forgotten the Mermaid who had neglected him, and if he thought of the Mer-folk at all it was as humans do, with wonder and with longing, and yet with fear.

Now the good old Stork who had first meddled in these matters kept one eye upon the doings in that neighborhood, and he had seen the sorrowful Mermaid wandering lonely up and down the shore. He knew it must be the Sea-child's mother, sorry at last for her long carelessness. As the years passed he began to pity the poor creature; but when he found himself growing too soft-hearted he would shake his head firmly and say to himself,—

"It will not do. She is not yet punished enough, for she was very cruel. If now she could have her baby again she would soon be as thoughtless as ever. Besides, there is my promise to Gil. So long as he keeps the secret so must I."

But one day, several years later, when the Stork was flying over the harbor, he spied the Mermaid lying upon a rock over which the waves dashed merrily, and she was weeping bitterly, tearing her lovely green hair. She looked so pretty and so forlorn that the bird's kind heart was touched, and he could not help stopping to comfort her a bit. Flying close to her head he said gently,—

"Poor Mermaid! What is the matter?"

"Oh, oh!" wailed the Mermaid. "Long, long ago I lost my pretty little Sea-child, and he is not to be found anywhere, anywhere in the whole sea, for I have looked. I have been from ocean to ocean, from pole to pole. Oh, what shall I do? He is on the land, I know he is, and the wicked humans are ill-treating him."

The Stork spoke slowly and gravely. "Was he so happy, then, in his sea-home? Did you love him and care for him very dearly?"

"No, no!" sobbed the Mermaid. "I did not love him enough. I did not make him happy. I neglected him and found him in the way, till one day he disappeared, and I shall never see him again. Oh, my baby, my little Sea-child!"

The Stork wiped a tear from his eye. "It is very sad," he said. "But perhaps it will comfort you to know that he is not far away."

"Oh!" cried the Mermaid, clasping her hands. "You know where he is? You will bring him back to me? Dear, dear Stork! I will give you a necklace of pearls and a necklace of coral if you will bring my baby to me again."

The Stork smiled grimly, looking down at his long neck. "A necklace of pearls and a necklace of coral!" he repeated. "How becoming they would be!" Then he grew grave once more and said: "I cannot return your child to you, but I can tell you something of him. He is indeed among the humans, but he is very happy there. They love him and he loves them, and all is well—so far."

"Oh, show him to me that I may take him away!" cried the Mermaid.

But the Stork shook his head. "No, no, for you deserted him," he said solemnly; "now he has another mother in yonder village who loves him better than you did. He has a brother, also, whom he loves best of all. You cannot claim him so long as he is happy there."

"Then shall I never see him again, wise Bird?" asked the Mermaid sadly.

"Perhaps," answered the Stork. "If he should become unhappy, or if the secret should be betrayed."

"Ah, then I must be again a cruel mother and hope that he may become unhappy," sobbed the Mermaid. "I shall look for him every day in the harbor near the village, and when his face is sad I shall claim him for my own."

"You will not know him," cried the Stork, rising on his wings and flapping away. "He wears a disguise. He is like a human,—like any other fisher-boy; and he bears a human name."

"Oh, tell me that name!" begged the Mermaid.

But the Stork only cried, "I must not tell. I have told too much already," and he was gone.

"Oh, then I will love all fisher-boys for his sake," sobbed the Mermaid as she dived down into the sea. "And someday, someday I shall find him out; for my baby is sure to be the finest of them all."

Now the years went by, and the parents of Gil and Jan were dead. The two brothers were tall and sturdy and stout, the finest lads in the whole country. But as their shadows grew taller and broader when they walked together across the sand, so another shadow which had begun to fall between them grew and grew. It was the shadow of Gil's selfishness and jealousy. So long as Jan was smaller and weaker than he, Gil was quite content, and never ceased to be grateful for the little brother who had come to be his playmate. But suddenly, as it seemed, he found that Jan was almost as big as himself; for the boy had thriven wondrously, though there were still several years which Jan could never make up. Gil was still the leader, but Jan was not far behind; and Jan himself led all the other boys when his brother was not by. Everyone loved Jan, for he was kind and merry, while Gil was often gloomy and disagreeable. Gil wanted to be first in everything, but there began to be some things that Jan could do better than he. It made Gil angry to hear his brother praised; it made him sulky and malicious, and sometimes he spoke unkindly to Jan, which caused the blue eyes to fill with tears. For, big fellow though he was, Jan was five years younger, and he was a sensitive lad, loving Gil more than anything else in the world. Gil's unkindness hurt Jan deeply, but could not make him love his brother less.

Both boys were famous swimmers. Gil was still the stronger of the two, and he could outswim any lad in town. As for Jan, the fishermen declared that he took to the water like a fish. No one in all the village could turn and twist, dive and glide and play such graceful pranks, flashing whitely through the waves, as did Jan. This was a great trouble to Gil, who wished to be foremost in this as in everything else. He was a selfish fellow; he had wanted a playmate to follow and admire him. He had not bargained for a comrade who might become a rival. And he seemed to love his brother less and less as the days went by.

One beautiful summer day Gil and Jan called together the other boys, the best swimmers in the village, and they all went down to the bay to swim. They played all sorts of water-games, in which the two brothers were leaders. They dived and floated and chased one another like fishes through the water. Jan, especially, won shouts of applause for his wonderful diving, for the other boys liked him, and were proud of him, glad to see him win. This again made Gil jealous and angry. Jan dived once more and remained under water so long that the boys began to fear that he would never come up; and in his wicked heart Gil half hoped that it was to be so. For it had come about that Gil began to wish he had no brother at all. So different was he from the boy who made the eager bargain with the good old Stork.

At last Jan's head came out of the water, bubbling and blowing, and the boys set up a cheer. Never before had any one in the village performed such a feat as that. But Jan did not answer their cheers with his usual merry laugh. Something was troubling him which made him look strange to the others. As soon as he reached the shore he ran up to Gil and whispered in his brother's ear a curious story.

"Oh, Gil!" he cried. "Such a strange feeling I have had! Down below there as I was swimming along I seemed to hear a strange sound like a cry, and then, surely, I felt something cling close to me, like soft arms. Gil, Gil, what could it have been? I have heard tell of the Mermaidens who are said to live in these waters. Some even say that they have seen them afar off on the rocks where the spray dashed highest. Gil, could it have been a Mermaid who touched me and seemed to pull me down as if to keep me under the water forever? I could hardly draw away, Gil. Tell me what you think it means?"

Gil was too angry at Jan's success to answer kindly. He sneered, remembering the secret which only he and the Stork knew.

"There are slimy folk, half fish and half human, people say. The less one has to do with them the better. I think you are half fish yourself, Jan. It is no credit to you that you are able to swim!" So spoke Gil, breaking the promise which he had once given.

On the minute came a hoarse cry overhead, and a great Stork flapped down the sky, fixing his sharp eyes upon Gil, as if in warning.

"Why, how strangely the Stork acts!" cried Jan.

Gil bit his lip and said no more, but from that moment he hated his brother wickedly, knowing that the Stork was still watching over the child whom he had taken from the sea.

But Jan had no time to ask Gil what he meant by the strange words which he had just spoken, for at that moment several of the boys came running up to them. "Ho, Gil! Ho, Jan!" they cried. "Let us have a race! Come, let us swim out to the Round Rock and back. And the winner of this race shall be champion of the village. Come, boys, make ready for the race!"

Gil's face brightened, for he had ever been the strongest swimmer on the bay, and now he could afford to be kind to poor Jan, whose blue eyes were clouded and unhappy, because of Gil's former harsh words and manner.

"Ho! The race, the race!" cried Gil. "Come, Jan, you can dive like a fish. Now let us see how you can swim. One, two, three! We are off!"

The boys sprang, laughing, into the water. Jan needed but a kind word from his brother to make him happy again. Off they started for the Round Rock, where the spray was dashing high.

The black heads bobbed up and down in the waves, drawing nearer and nearer to the rock. Gradually they separated, and some fell behind. The lads could not all keep up the lively strokes with which they had begun the race. Four held the lead; Boise and Cadoc, the lighthouse-keeper's sons, Gil, and Jan.

Almost abreast they rounded the rock, and began the long stretch back to the beach. Soon Boise began to fall behind. In a little while Cadoc's strength failed also. They shouted, laughingly, that they were fairly beaten, and those who were on shore began to cry encouragement to the two brothers, who alone were left in the race.

"Gil! Jan! Oh, Gil! Oh, Jan! Hasten, lads, for one of you is the champion. Hurrah! Hurrah!"

Gil was in high spirits, for he was still in the lead. "Hurry, little brother," he cried, "or I shall beat you badly. Oho! You can dive, but that is scarcely swimming, my fine lad. You had better hurry, or I win."

And Jan did hurry. He put forth all his strength as he had never done before. Soon the black heads bobbed side by side in the water, and Gil ceased to laugh and jest, for it was now a struggle in good earnest. He shut his teeth angrily, straining forward with all his might. But push as he would, Jan kept close beside. At last, when within a few yards of the beach, Jan gave a little laughing shout and shot through the water like a flash. He had been saving his strength for this,—and he had won!

The other boys dragged him up the beach with shouts and cheers of welcome to the new champion, while Gil, who had borne that title for so long, crawled ashore unaided.

"Hurrah for Jan!" they cried, tossing their caps and dancing happily, for Jan was a great favorite. "Hurrah for the little brother! Now Gil must take the second place. You are the big brother now!" And they laughed and jeered at Gil,—not maliciously, but because they were pleased with Jan.

Jan ran to Gil and held out his hand for his brother's congratulations, but Gil thrust it aside. "It was not a fair race!" he sputtered. "Unfair, unfair, I vow!"

The others gathered around, surprised to see Gil so angry and with such wild eyes.

"Gil, oh, Gil! What do you mean?" cried Jan, turning very pale. "Why was it not a fair race, brother?"

"Brother! You are no brother of mine!" shouted Gil, beside himself with rage. "You are a changeling,—half fish, half sea-monster. You were helped in this race by the sea-people; you cannot deny it. I saw one push you to the shore. You could not have beaten me else. Everyone knows that I am the better swimmer, though I am no fish."

"Nonsense!" cried Boise, clapping Gil on the shoulder with a laugh. "You talk foolishness, Gil. There are no sea-folk in these waters; those are old women's tales. It was a fair race, I say, and Jan is our champion."

But Jan heeded only the cruel words which his brother had spoken. "Gil, what do you mean?" he asked again, trembling with a new fear. "I was not helped by any one."

"Ha!" cried Gil, pointing at him fiercely, "see him tremble, see his guilty looks! He knows that I speak true. The Mermaid helped him. He is half fish. He came out of the sea and was no real brother of mine, but a Merbaby. A Mermaid was his mother!"

At these words a whirring sound was heard in the air overhead, and a second time the Stork appeared, flapping across the scene out to sea, where he alighted upon the Round Rock. But Gil was too angry even to notice him.

"Gil, Gil, tell me how this can be?" begged Jan, going up to his brother and laying a pleading hand upon his arm.

But Gil shook him off, crying, "It is true! He is half fish and the sea-folk helped him. It was not a fair race. Let us try it again."

"Nonsense!" cried the other boys indignantly. "It was a fair race. Jan need not try again, for he is our champion. We will have it so."

But Jan was looking at Gil strangely, and the light was gone out of his eyes. His face was very white. "I did not know that you cared so much to win," he said to Gil in a low voice. Then he turned to the others. "If my brother thinks it was not a fair race let us two try again. Let us swim once more to the Round Rock and back; and the winner shall be declared the village champion."

For Jan meant this time to let his brother beat. What did he care about anything now, since Gil hated him so much that he could tell that story?

"Well, let them try the race again, since Jan will have it so," cried the boys, grumbling and casting scornful looks at Gil, who had never been so unpopular with them as at this moment.

Once more the two sprang into the waves and started for the Round Rock, where the spray was dashing merrily over the plumage of the Stork as he stood there upon one leg, trying not to mind the wetness which he hated. For he was talking earnestly with a pretty Mermaid who sat on the rock in the surf, wringing her hands.

"It is he! It is he!" she cried. "I know him now. It is the lad whom they call Jan, the finest swimmer of them all. Oh, he dives like a fish! He swims like a true Sea-child. He is my own baby, my little one! I followed, I watched him. I could hardly keep my hands from him. Tell me, dear Stork, is he not indeed my own?"

The Stork looked at her gravely. "It is no longer a secret," he said, "for Jan has been betrayed. He who is now Jan the unhappy mortal boy was once your unhappy Sea-baby."

"Unhappy! Oh, is he unhappy?" cried the Mermaid. "Then at last I may claim him as you promised. I may take him home once more to our fair sea-home, to cherish him and make him happier than he ever was in all his little life. But tell me, dear Stork, will he not be my own little Sea-child again? I would not have him in his strange, ugly human guise, but as my own little fish-tailed baby."

"When you kiss him," said the Stork, "when you throw your arms about his neck and speak to him in the sea-language, he will become a Sea-child once more, as he was when I found him in his cradle on the rocks. But look! Yonder he comes. A second race has begun, and they swim this way. Wait until they have turned the rock, and then it will be your turn. Ah, Gil! You have ill kept your promise to me!"

Yes, the race between the brothers was two thirds over. Side by side as before the two black heads pushed through the waves. Both faces were white and drawn, and there was no joy in either. Gil's was pale with anger, Jan's only with sadness. He loved his brother still, but he knew that Gil loved him no more.

They were nearing the shore where the boys waited breathlessly for the end of this strange contest. Suddenly Jan turned his face towards Gil and gave him one look. "You will win, brother," he breathed brokenly, "my strength is failing. You are the better swimmer, after all. Tell the lads that I confess it. Go on and come in as the champion."

He thought that Gil might turn to see whether he needed aid. But Gil made no sign save to quicken his strokes, which had begun to lag, for in truth he was very weary. He pushed on with only a desire to win the shore and to triumph over his younger brother. With a sigh Jan saw him shoot ahead, then turning over on his back he began to float carelessly. He would not make another effort. It was then that he saw the Stork circling close over his head; and it did not seem so very strange when the Stork said to him,—

"Swim, Jan! You are the better swimmer; you can beat him yet."

"I know; but I do not wish to beat," said Jan wearily. "He would only hate me the more."

"There is one who loves you more than ever he did," said the Stork gently.

"Will you go home to your sea-mother, the beautiful Mermaid?"

"The Mermaid!" cried Jan; "then it is true. My real home is not upon the shore?"

"Your real home is here, in the waves. Beneath them your mother waits."

"Then I need not go back to that other home," said Jan, "that home where I am hated?"

"Ah, you will be loved in this sea-home," said the Stork. "You will be very happy there. Come, come, Mermaid! Kiss your child and take him home."

Then Jan felt two soft arms come around his neck and two soft lips pressed upon his own. "Dear child!" whispered a soft voice, "come with me to your beautiful sea-home and be happy always."

A strange, drowsy feeling came over him, and he forgot how to be sad. He felt himself growing younger and younger. The world beyond the waves looked unreal and odd. He forgot why he was there; he forgot the race, the boys, Gil, and all his trouble. But instead he began to remember things of a wonderful dream. He closed his eyes; the sea rocked him gently, as in a cradle, and slowly, slowly, with the soft arms of the Mermaid about him, and her green hair twining through his fingers, he sank down through the water.

As he sank the likeness of a human boy faded from him, and he became once more a fresh, fair little Sea-child, with a scaly tail and plump, merry face. The Mer-folk came to greet him. The fishes darted about him playfully. The sea-anemones beckoned him with enticing fingers. The Sea-child was at home again, and the sea was kind.

So Gil became the champion; but that was little pleasure to him, as you can fancy. For he remembered, he remembered, and he could not forget. He thought, like all the village, that Jan had been drowned through his brother's selfishness and jealousy. He forgave himself less even than the whole village could forgive him for the loss of their favorite; for he knew better than they how much more he was to blame, because he had broken the promise which kept Jan by him. If he had known how happy the Sea-child now was in the home from which he had come to be Gil's brother, perhaps Gil would not have lived thereafter so sad a life. The Stork might have told him the truth. But the wise old Stork would not. That was to be Gil's punishment,—to remember and regret and to reproach himself always for the selfishness and jealousy which had cost him a loving brother.

The Mermaid of Knockdolion

GEORGE DOUGLAS
ILLUSTRATIONS KARL WILHELM DIEFENBACH

The old house of Knockdolion stood near the water of Girvan, with a black stone at the end of it. A mermaid used to come from the water at night, and taking her seat upon this stone, would sing for hours, at the same time combing her long yellow hair. The lady of Knockdolion found that this serenade was an annoyance to her baby, and she thought proper to attempt getting quit of it, by causing the stone to be broken by her servants. The mermaid, coming next night, and finding her favourite seat gone, sang thus:

"Ye may think on your cradle—I'll think on my stane;
And there'll never be an heir to Knockdolion again."

Soon after, the cradle was found overturned, and the baby dead under it. It is added that the family soon after became extinct.

Lutey and the Mermaid

MABEL QUILLER COUCH

ILLUSTRATIONS JOHN REINHARD WEGUELIN

One lovely summer evening many, many years ago, an old man named Lutey was standing on the seashore not far from that beautiful bit of coast called the Lizard. On the edge of the cliff above him stood a small farm, and here he lived, spending his time between farming, fishing, and, we must admit it, smuggling, too, whenever he got a chance. This summer evening he had finished his day's work early, and while waiting for his supper he strolled along the sands a little way, to see if there was any wreckage to

183

be seen, for it was long since he had had any luck in that way, and he was very much put out about it.

This evening, though, he was no luckier than he had been before, and he was turning away, giving up his search as hopeless, when from somewhere out seaward came a long, low, wailing cry. It was not the melancholy cry of a gull, but of a woman or child in distress.

Lutey stopped, and listened, and looked back, but, as far as he could see, not a living creature was to be seen on the beach but himself. Even though while he listened the sound came wailing over the sand again, and this time left no doubt in his mind. It was a voice. Someone was in trouble, evidently, and calling for help.

Far out on the sands rose a group of rocks which, though covered at high water, were bare now. It was about half ebb, and spring tide, too, so the sea was further out than usual, so far, in fact, that a wide bar of sand stretched between the rocks and the sea. It was from these rocks that the cry seemed to come, and Lutey, feeling sure that someone was out there in distress, turned and walked back quickly to see if he could give any help.

As he drew near he saw that there was no one on the landward side, so he hurried round to the seaward,—

and there, to his amazement, his eyes met a sight which left him almost speechless!

Lying on a ledge at the base of the rock, partially covered by the long seaweed which grew in profusion over its rough sides, and partially by her own hair, which was the most glorious you can possibly imagine, was the most beautiful woman his eyes had ever lighted upon. Her skin was a delicate pink and white, even more beautiful than those exquisite little shells one picks up sometimes on the seashore, her clear green eyes sparkled and flashed like the waves with the sun on them, while her hair was the colour of rich gold, like the sun in its glory, and with a ripple in it such as one sees on the sea on a calm day.

This wonderful creature was gazing mournfully out at the distant sea, and uttering from time to time the pitiful cry which had first attracted Lutey's attention. She was evidently in great distress, but how to offer her help and yet not frighten her he knew not, for the roar of the sea had deadened the sound of his footsteps on the soft sand, and she was quite unconscious of his presence.

Lutey coughed and hem'd, but it was of no use—she could not or did not hear; he stamped, he kicked the rock, but all in vain, and at last he had to go close to her and speak.

"What's the matter, missie?" he said. "What be doing all out here by yourself?" He spoke as gently as possible, but, in spite of his gentleness, the lovely creature shrieked with terror, and diving down into the deep pool at the base of the rock, disappeared entirely.

At first Lutey thought she had drowned herself, but when he looked closely into the pool, and contrived to peer through the cloud of hair which floated like fine seaweed all over the top of it, he managed to distinguish a woman's head and shoulders underneath, and looking closer he saw, he was sure, a fish's tail! His knees quaked under him, at that sight, for he realized that the lovely lady was no other than a mermaid!

She, though, seemed as frightened as he was, so he summoned up his courage to speak to her again, for it is always wise to be kind to mermaids, and to avoid offending them, for if they are angry there is no knowing what harm they may do to you.

"Don't be frightened, lady," he said coaxingly; "I wouldn't hurt 'ee for the world, I wouldn't harm a living creature. I only wants to know what your trouble is."

While he was speaking, the maiden had raised her head slightly above the water, and now was gazing at him with eyes the like of which he had never seen before. "I 'opes she understands Carnish," he added to himself, "for 'tis the only langwidge I'm fluent in."

"Beautiful sir," she replied in answer to his thoughts, "we sea-folk can understand all languages, for we visit the coast of every land, and all the tribes of the world sail over our kingdom, and oft-times come down through the waters to our home. The greatest kindness you can do me is to go away. You are accustomed to women who walk, covered with silks and laces. We could not wear such in our world, sporting in the waves, swimming into caverns, clambering into sunken ships. You cannot realize our free and untrammelled existence."

"Now, my lovely lady," said old Lutey, who did not understand a half of what she was saying, "don't 'ee think anything about such trifles, but stop your tears and tell me what I can do for 'ee. For, for sure, I can help 'ee somehow. Tell me how you come'd here, and where you wants to get to."

So the fair creature floated higher in the water, and, gradually growing braver, she presently climbed up and perched herself on the rock where Lutey had first seen her. Her long hair fell about her like a glorious mantle, and she needed no other, for it quite covered her. Holding in her hand her comb and mirror, and glancing from time to time at the latter, she told the old man her story.

"Only a few hours ago," she said sadly, "I was sporting about with my husband and children, as happy as a mermaiden could be. At length, growing weary, we all retired to rest in one of the caverns at Kynance, and there on a soft couch of seaweed my husband laid himself down to sleep. The children went off to play, and I was left alone. For some time I watched the crabs playing in the water, or the tiny fish at the bottom of the pools, but the sweet scent of flowers came to me from the gardens of your world, borne on the light breeze, and I felt I must go and see what these flowers were like whose breath was so beautiful, for we have nothing like it in our dominions. Exquisite sea-plants we have, but they have no sweet perfume.

"Seeing that my husband was asleep, and the children quite happy and safe, I swam off to this shore, but when here I found I could not get near the flowers; I could see them on the tops of the cliffs far, far beyond my reach, so I thought I would rest here for a time, and dress my hair, while breathing in their sweetness.

"I sat on, dreaming of your world and trying to picture to myself what it was like, until I awoke with a start to find the tide far out, beyond the bar. I was so frightened I screamed to my husband to come and help me, but even if he heard me he could not get to me over that sandy ridge; and if he wakes before I am back, and misses me, he will be so angry, for he is very jealous. He will be hungry, too, and if he finds no supper prepared he will eat some of the children!"

"Oh, my dear!" cried Lutey, quite horrified, "he surely wouldn't never do such a dreadful thing!"

"Ah, you do not know Mermen," she said sorrowfully. "They are such gluttons, and will gobble up their children in a moment if their meals are a little late. Scores of my children have been taken from me. That is how it is," she explained, "that you do not oftener see us sea-folk. Poor children, they never learn wisdom! Directly their father begins to whistle or sing, they crowd about him, they are so fond of music, and he gets them to come and kiss his cheek, or whisper in his ear, then he opens wide his mouth, and in they go.—Oh dear, what shall I do! I have only ten little ones left, and they will all be gone if I don't get home before he wakes!"

"Don't 'ee take on so, my dear. The tide will soon be in, and then you can float off as quick as you like."

"Oh, but I cannot wait," she cried, tears running down her cheeks. "Beautiful mortal, help me! Carry me out to sea, give me your aid for ten minutes only, and I will make you rich and glorious for life. Ask of me anything you want, and it shall be yours."

Lutey was so enthralled by the loveliness of the mermaid, that he stood gazing at her, lost in wonder. Her voice, which sounded like a gentle murmuring stream, was to him the most lovely music he had ever heard. He was so fascinated that he would have done anything she asked him. He stooped to pick her up.

"First of all, take this," she said, giving him her pearl comb, "take this, to prove to you that you have not been dreaming, gentle stranger, and that I will do for you what I have said. When you want me, comb the sea three times with this, and call me by my name, 'Morwenna,' and I will come to you. Now take me to the sea."

Stooping again he picked her up in his arms. She clung tightly to him, twining her long, cool arms around his neck, until he felt half suffocated. "Tell me your wishes," she said sweetly, as they went along; "you shall have three. Riches will, of course, be one."

"No, lady," said Lutey thoughtfully, "I don't know that I'm so set on getting gold, but I'll tell 'ee what I should like. I'd dearly love to be able to remove the spells of the witches, to have power over the spirits to make them tell me all I want to know, and I'd like to be able to cure diseases."

"You are the first unselfish man I have met," cried the mermaid admiringly, "you shall have your wishes, and, in addition, I promise you as a reward, that your family shall never come to want."

In a state of great delight, Lutey trudged on with his lovely burthen, while she chatted gaily to him of her home, of the marvels and the riches of the sea, and the world that lay beneath it.

"Come with me, noble youth," she cried, "come with me to our caves and palaces; there are riches, beauty, and everything mortal can want. Our homes are magnificent, the roofs are covered with diamonds and other gems, so that it is ever light and sparkling, the walls are of amber and coral. Your floors are of rough, ugly rocks, ours are of mother-of-pearl. For statuary we have the bodies of earth's most beautiful sons and daughters, who come to us in ships, sent by the King of the Storms. We embalm them, so that they look more lovely even than in life, with their eyes still sparkling, their lips of ruby-red, and the delicate pink of the sea-shell in their cheeks. Come and see for yourself how well we care for them, and how reposeful they look in their pearl and coral homes, with sea-plants growing around them, and gold and silver heaped at their feet. They crossed the world to get it, and their journeys have not been failures. Will you come, noble stranger? Come to be one of us whose lives are all love, and sunshine, and merriment?"

"None of it's in my line, I'm thinking, my dear," said Lutey. "I'd rather come across some of the things that have gone down in the wrecks, wines and brandy, laces and silks; there's a pretty sight of it all gone to the bottom, one time and another, I'm thinking."

"Ah yes! We have vast cellars full of the choicest wines ever made, and caves stored with laces and silks. Come, stranger, come, and take all you want."

"Well," answered the old smuggler, who was thinking what a fine trade he could do, if only he could reach those caves and cellars, "I must say I'd like to, 'tis very tempting, but I should never live to get there, I'm thinking. I should be drowned or smothered before I'd got half-way."

"No, oh no, I can manage that for you. I will make two slits under your chin, your lovely countenance will not suffer, for your beard will hide them. Such a pair of gills is all you want, so do not fear. Do not leave me, generous-hearted youth. Come to the mermaid's home!" They were in the sea by this time, and the breakers they wanted to reach were not far off. Lutey felt strangely tempted to go with this Siren; her flashing green eyes had utterly bewitched him by this time, and her promises had turned his head. She saw that he was almost consenting, almost in her power. She clasped her long, wet, finny fingers more closely round his neck, and pressed her cool lips to his cheeks.

Another instant, and Lutey would have gone to his doom, but at that moment there came from the shore the sound of a dog barking as though in distress. It was the barking of Lutey's own dog, a great favourite with its master. Lutey turned to look. At the edge of the water the poor creature stood; evidently frantic to follow its master, it dashed into the sea and out again, struggling, panting. Beyond, on the cliff, stood his home, the windows flaming against the sun, his garden, and the country round looking green and beautiful; the smoke was rising from his chimney, — ah, his supper! The thought of his nice hot meal broke the spell, and he saw his danger.

"Let me go, let me go!" he shrieked, trying to lower the mermaid to the ground. She only clung the more tightly to him. He felt a sudden fear and loathing of the creature with the scaly body, and fish's tail. Her green eyes no longer fascinated him. He remembered all the tales he had heard of the power of mermaids, and their wickedness, and grew more and more terrified.

"Let me go!" he yelled again, "unwind your gashly great tail from about my legs, and your skinny fingers from off my throat, or I'll—I'll kill you!" and with the same he whipped his big clasp-knife from his pocket.

As the steel flashed before the mermaid's eyes she slipped from him and swam slowly away, but as she went she sang, and the words floated back to Lutey mournfully yet threateningly. "Farewell, farewell for nine long years. Then, my love, I will come again. Mine, mine, forever mine!"

Poor Lutey, greatly relieved to see her disappear beneath the waves, turned and waded slowly back to land, but so shaken and upset was he by all that had happened, that it was almost more than he could accomplish. On reaching the shore he just managed to scramble to the shed where he kept many of the treasures he had smuggled from time to time, but having reached it he dropped down in a deep, overpowering sleep.

Poor old Ann Betty Lutey was in a dreadful state of mind when supper-time came and went and her husband had not returned. He had never missed it before. All through the night she watched anxiously for him, but when breakfast-time came, and still there was no sign of him, she could not rest at home another minute, and started right away in search of him.

She did not have to search far, though. Outside the door of the shed she found the dog lying sleeping, and as the dog was seldom seen far from his master, she thought she would search the shed first,—and there, of course, she found her husband.

He was still sound asleep. Ann Betty, vexed at once at having been frightened for nothing, shook him none too gently. "Here, Lutey, get up to once, do you hear!" she cried crossly. "Why ever didn't 'ee come in to supper,—such a beautiful bit of roast as I'd got, too! Where've 'ee been? What 'ave 'ee been doing? What 'ave 'ee been sleeping here for?"

Lutey raised himself into a sitting position. "Who are you?" he shouted. "Are you the beautiful maiden come for me? Are you Morwenna?"

"Whatever are you talking about? You haven't called me beautiful for the last thirty years, and I ain't called Morwenna. I'm Ann Betty Lutey, your own lawful wife, and if you don't know me, you must be gone clean out of your mind."

"Ann Betty Lutey," said the old man solemnly, "if you're my lawful wife you've had a narrow escape this night of being left a widow woman, and you may be thankful you've ever set eyes on me again."

"Come in and have some breakfast," said Ann Betty Lutey sternly, "and if you ain't better then I'll send for the doctor. It's my belief your brain is turned."

Lutey got up obediently and went in to his breakfast; indeed, he was glad enough of it, for he was light-headed from want of food. His breakfast did him good. Before he had finished it he was able to tell his wife about his adventure the night before, and he told it so gravely and sensibly that Ann Betty believed every word of it, and no longer thought his brain was turned.

Indeed, she was so much impressed by his story that before many hours had passed she had gone round to every house in the parish spreading the news, and to prove the truth of it she produced the pearl comb.

Then, oh dear, the gossiping that went on! It really was dreadful! The women neglected their homes, their children, and everything else for the whole of that week; and for months after old Lutey was besieged by all the sick and sorry for miles and miles around, who came to him to be cured. He did such a big business in healing people, that not a doctor for miles round could earn a living. Everyone went to old Lutey, and when it was found that he had power over witchcraft, too, he became the most important man in the whole country.

Lutey had been so rude and rough to the mermaiden when he parted from her, that no one would have been surprised if she had avenged herself on him somehow, and punished him severely. But no, she was true to all her promises. He got all his wishes, and neither he nor his descendants have ever come to want. Better far, though, would it have been for him had it been otherwise, for he paid dearly enough for his wishes in the end.

Nine years from that very time, on a calm moonlight night, Lutey, forgetting all about the mermaid and her threats, arranged to go out with a friend to do a little fishing. There was not a breath of wind stirring, and the sea was like glass, so that a sail was useless, and they had to take to the oars. Suddenly, though, without any puff of wind, or anything else to cause it, the sea rose round the boat in one huge wave, covered with a thick crest of foam, and in the midst of the foam was Morwenna!

Morwenna! as lovely as ever, her arms outstretched, her clear green eyes fixed steadily, triumphantly on Lutey. She did not open her lips, or make a sign, she only gazed and gazed at her victim.

For a moment he looked at her as though bewildered, then like one bereft of his senses by some spell, he rose in the boat, and turned his face towards the open sea. "My time is come," he said solemnly and sadly, and without another word to his frightened companion he sprang out of the boat and joined the mermaid. For a yard or two they swam in silence side by side, then disappeared beneath the waves, and the sea was as smooth again as though nothing had happened.

From that moment poor Lutey has never been seen, nor has his body been found. Probably he now forms one of the pieces of statuary so prized by the mermaiden, and stands decked with sea-blossoms, with gold heaped at his feet. Or, maybe, with a pair of gills slit under his chin, he swims about in their beautiful palaces, and revels in the cellars of shipwrecked wines. The misfortunes to his family did not end, though, with Lutey's disappearance, for, no matter how careful they are, how far they live from the sea, or what precautions they take to protect themselves, every ninth year one of old Lutey's descendants is claimed by the sea.

Melusina

SABINE BARING-GOULD

ILLUSTRATIONS JULIUS HUBNER (COVER), ÉMILE BAYARD

E mmerick, Count of Poitou, was a nobleman of great wealth, and eminent for his virtues. He had two children, a son named Bertram, and a daughter Blaniferte. In the great forest which stretched away in all directions around the knoll on which stood the town and castle of Poictiers, lived a Count de la Forêt, related to Emmerick, but poor and with a large family. Out of compassion for his kinsman, the Count of Poitou adopted his youngest son Raymond, a beautiful and amiable youth, and made him his constant companion in hall and in the chase.

One day the Count and his retinue hunted a boar in the forest of Colombiers, and distancing his servants, Emmerick found himself alone in the depths of the wood with Raymond. The boar had escaped. Night came on, and the two huntsmen lost their way. They succeeded in lighting a fire, and were warming themselves over the blaze, when suddenly the boar plunged out of the forest upon the Count, and Raymond, snatching up his sword, struck at the beast, but the blade glanced off and slew the Count. A second blow laid the boar at his side. Raymond then with horror perceived that his friend and master was dead. In despair he mounted his horse and fled, not knowing whither he went.

Presently the boughs of the trees became less interlaced, and the trunks fewer; next moment his horse, crashing through the shrubs, brought him out on a pleasant glade, white with rime, and illumined by the new moon; in the midst bubbled up a limpid fountain, and flowed away over a pebbly floor with a soothing murmur. Near the fountainhead sat three maidens in glimmering white dresses, with long waving golden hair, and faces of inexpressible beauty.

Raymond was riveted to the spot with astonishment. He believed that he saw a vision of angels, and would have prostrated himself at their feet, had not one of them advanced and stayed him. The lady inquired the cause of his manifest terror, and the young man, after a slight hesitation, told her of his dreadful misfortune. She listened with attention, and at the conclusion of his story, recommended him to remount his horse, and gallop out of the forest, and return to Poictiers, as though unconscious of what had taken place. All the huntsmen had that day lost themselves in the wood, and were returning singly, at intervals, to the castle, so that no suspicion would attach to him. The body of the count would be found, and from the proximity of the dead boar, it would be concluded that he had fallen before the tusk of the animal, to which he had given its death-blow.

Relieved of his anxiety, Raymond was able to devote his attention exclusively to the beauty of the lady who addressed him, and found means to prolong the conversation till daybreak. He had never beheld charms equal to hers, and the susceptible heart of the youth was completely captivated by the fair unknown. Before he left her, he obtained from her a promise to be his. She then told him to ask of his kinsman Bertram, as a gift, so much ground around the fountain where they had met, as could be covered by a stag's hide: upon this ground she undertook to erect a magnificent palace. Her name, she told him, was Melusina; she was a water-fay of great power and wealth. His she consented to be, but subject to one condition, that her Saturdays might be spent in a complete seclusion, upon which he should never venture to intrude.

Raymond then left her, and followed her advice to the letter. Bertram, who succeeded his father, readily granted the land he asked for, but was not a little vexed, when he found that, by cutting the hide into threads, Raymond had succeeded in making it include a considerable area.

Raymond then invited the young count to his wedding, and the marriage festivities took place, with unusual splendour, in the magnificent castle erected by Melusina. On the evening of the marriage, the bride, with tears in her beautiful eyes, implored her husband on no account to attempt an intrusion on her privacy upon Saturdays, for such an intrusion must infallibly separate them for ever. The enamoured Raymond readily swore to strictly observe her wishes in this matter.

Melusina continued to extend the castle, and strengthen its fortifications, till the like was not to be seen in all the country round. On its completion she named it after herself Lusinia, a name which has been corrupted into Lusignan, which it bears to this day.

In course of time, the Lady of Lusignan gave birth to a son, who was baptized Urian. He was a strangely shaped child: his mouth was large, his ears pendulous; one of his eyes was red, the other green.

A year later she gave birth to another son, whom she called Cedes; he had a face which was scarlet. In thank-offering for his birth she erected and endowed the convent of Malliers; and, as a place of residence for her child, built the strong castle of Favent.

Melusina then bore a third son, who was christened Gyot. He was a fine, handsome child, but one of his eyes was higher up in his face than the other. For him his mother built La Rochelle.

Her next son Anthony, had long claws on his fingers, and was covered with hair; the next again had but a single eye. The sixth was Geoffry with the Tooth, so called from a boar's tusk which protruded from his jaw. Other children she had, but all were in some way disfigured and monstrous.

Years passed, and the love of Raymond for his beautiful wife never languished. Every Saturday she left him, and spent the twenty-four hours in the strictest seclusion, without her husband thinking of intruding on her privacy. The children grew up to be great heroes and illustrious warriors. One, Freimund, entered the Church, and became a pious monk, in the abbey of Malliers. The aged Count de la Forêt and the brothers of Raymond shared in his good fortune, and the old man spent his last years in the castle with his son, whilst the brothers were furnished with money and servants suitable to their rank.

One Saturday, the old father inquired at dinner after his daughter-in-law. Raymond replied that she was not visible on Saturdays. Thereupon one of his brothers, drawing him aside, whispered that strange gossiping tales were about relative to this sabbath seclusion, and that it behoved him to inquire into it, and set the minds of people at rest. Full of wrath and anxiety, the count rushed off to the private apartments of the countess, but found them empty. One door alone was locked, and that opened into a bath. He looked through the keyhole, and to his dismay beheld her in the water, her lower extremities changed into the tail of a monstrous fish or serpent.

Silently he withdrew. No word of what he had seen passed his lips; it was not loathing that filled his heart, but anguish at the thought that by his fault he must lose the beautiful wife who had been the charm and glory of his life. Some time passed by, however, and Melusina gave no token of consciousness that she had been observed duringthe period of her transformation. But one day news reached the castle that Geoffry with the Tooth had attacked the monastery of Malliers, and

"Away, odious serpent, contaminator of my honourable race!"

burned it; and that in the flames had perished
Freimund, with the abbot and a hundred monks. On
hearing of this disaster, the poor father, in a paroxysm
of misery, exclaimed, as Melusina approached to
comfort him, "Away, odious serpent, contaminator of
my honourable race!"

At these words she fainted; and Raymond, full of
sorrow for having spoken thus intemperately, strove
to revive her. When she came to herself again, with
streaming tears she kissed and embraced him for the

last time. "O husband!" she said, "I leave two little ones in their cradle; look tenderly after them, bereaved of their mother. And now farewell forever! yet know that thou, and those who succeed thee, shall see me hover over this fair castle of Lusignan, whenever a new lord is to come." And with a long wail of agony she swept from the window, leaving the impression of her foot on the stone she last touched.

The children in arms she had left were Dietrich and Raymond. At night, the nurses beheld a glimmering figure appear near the cradle of the babes, most like the vanished countess, but from her waist downwards terminating in a scaly fish-tail enamelled blue and white. At her approach the little ones extended their arms and smiled, and she took them to her breast and suckled them; but as the grey dawn stole in at the casement, she vanished, and the children's cries told the nurses that their mother was gone.

The Princess of the Tung-t'ing Lake

HERBET A. GILES FROM THE ORIGINAL BY P'U SUNG-LING

ILLUSTRATIONS KATSUSHIKA HOKUSAI

C h'en Pi-Chiao was a Pekingese; and being a poor man he attached himself as secretary to the suite of a high military official named Chia. On one occasion, while anchored on the Tung-t'ing lake, they saw a dolphin floating on the surface of the water; and General Chia took his bow and shot at it, wounding the creature in the back. A fish was hanging on to its tail, and would not let go; so both were pulled out of the water together, and attached to the mast.

The fish laying there opening its mouth as if pleading for life, until at length young Ch'en begged the General to let them go again; and then he himself half-jokingly put a piece of plaster upon the dolphin's wound, and had the two thrown back into the water, where they were seen for some time afterwards diving and rising again to the surface.

About a year after, Ch'en was once more crossing the Tung-t'ing lake on his way home, when the boat was upset in a squall, and he himself was saved only by clinging to a bamboo crate, which finally, after floating about all night, caught in the over- hanging branch of a tree, and thus enabled him to scramble on shore. By-and-by, another body floated in, and this turned out to be his servant; but on dragging him out, he found the servant was already dead. In great distress, he sat himself down to rest, and saw beautiful green hills and waving willows, but not a single human being of whom he could ask the way. From early dawn till the morning was far advanced he remained in that state; and then, thinking he saw his servant's body move, he stretched out his hand to feel it, and before long the man threw up several quarts of water and recovered his consciousness. They now dried their clothes in the sun, and by noon these were fit to put on; at which period the pangs of hunger began to assail them, and accordingly they started over the hills in the hope of coming upon other men.

As they were walking along, an arrow whizzed past, and the next moment two young ladies dashed by on handsome palfreys. Each had a scarlet band round her head, with a bunch of pheasant's feathers stuck in her hair, and wore a purple riding-jacket with small sleeves, confined by a green embroidered girdle round the waist. One of them carried a cross-bow for shooting bullets, and the other had on her arm a dark-coloured bow-and-arrow case. Reaching the brow of the hill, Ch'en beheld a number of riders engaged in beating the surrounding cover, all of whom were beautiful girls and dressed exactly alike. Afraid to advance any further, he inquired of a youth who appeared to be in attendance, and the latter told him that it was a hunting party from the palace; and then, having supplied him with food from his wallet, he bade him retire quickly, adding that if he fell in with them he would assuredly be put to death.

Thereupon Ch'en hurried away; and descending the hill, turned into a thicket of trees where there was a building which he thought would be a monastery. On getting nearer, he saw that the place was surrounded by a wall, and between him and a half- open red-door was a brook spanned by a stone bridge leading up to it. Pulling back the door, he beheld within a number of ornamental buildings circling in the air like so many clouds, and for all the world resembling the Imperial pleasure-grounds; and thinking it must be the park of some official personage, he walked quietly in, enjoying the delicious fragrance of the flowers as he pushed aside the thick vegetation which obstructed his way. After traversing a winding path fenced in by balustrades, Ch'en reached a second enclosure, wherein were a quantity of tall willow-trees which swept the red eaves of the buildings with their branches. The note of some bird would set the petals of the flowers fluttering in the air, and the least wind would bring the seed-vessels down from the elm-trees above; and the effect upon the eye and heart of the beholder was something quite unknown in the world of mortals.

Passing through a small kiosk, Ch'en and his servant came upon a swing which seemed as though suspended from the clouds, while the ropes hung idly down in the utter stillness that prevailed. Thinking by this that they were approaching the ladies' apartments, Ch'en would have turned back, but at that moment he heard sounds of horses' feet at the door, and what seemed to be the laughter of a bevy of girls. So he and his servant hid themselves in a bush ; and by-and-by, as the sounds came nearer, he heard one of the young ladies say, "We've had but poor sport today;" whereupon another cried out, "If the princess hadn't shot that wild goose, we should have taken all this trouble for nothing."

Shortly after this, a number of girls dressed in red came in escorting a young lady, who went and sat down. She wore a hunting costume with tight sleeves, and was about fourteen or fifteen years old. Her hair looked like a cloud of mist at the back of her head, and her waist seemed as though a breath of wind might snap it incomparable for beauty, even among the celebrities of old. Just then the attendants handed her some exquisitely fragrant tea, and stood glittering round her like a bank of beautiful embroidery.

In a few moments the young lady arose and descended the kiosk; at which one of her attendants cried out, "Is your Highness too fatigued by riding to take a turn in the swing?" The princess replied that she was not; and immediately some supported her under the shoulders, while others seized her arms, and others again arranged her petticoats, and brought her the proper shoes. Thus they helped her into the swing, she herself stretching out her shining arms, and putting her feet into a suitable pair of slippers ; and then away she went, light as a flying-swallow, far up into the fleecy clouds. As soon as she had had enough, the attendants helped her out, and one of them exclaimed, "Truly, your Highness is a perfect angel!" At this the young lady laughed, and walked away, Ch'en gazing after her in a state of semi-consciousness, until, at length, the voices died away, and he and his servant crept forth.

Walking up and down near the swing, he suddenly spied a red handkerchief near the paling, which he knew had been dropped by one of the young ladies; and, thrusting it joyfully into his sleeve, he walked up and entered the kiosk. There, upon a table, lay writing materials, and taking out the handkerchief he composed upon it the following lines: "What form divine was just now sporting nigh? 'Twas she, I trow of 'golden lily' fame; Her charms the moon's fair denizens might shame, Her fairy footsteps bear her to the sky." Humming this stanza to himself, Ch'en walked along seeking for the path by which he had entered; but every door was securely barred, and he knew not what to do. So he went back to the kiosk, when suddenly one of the young ladies appeared, and asked him in astonishment what he did there. "I have lost my way," replied Ch'en; "I pray you lend me your assistance."

"Truly, your Highness is a perfect angel!"

"Do you happen to have found a red handkerchief?" said the girl. "I have, indeed," answered Ch'en, "but I fear I have made it somewhat dirty;" and, suiting the action to the word, he drew it forth, and handed it to her. "Wretched man!" cried the young lady, "you are undone. This is a handkerchief the princess is constantly using, and you have gone and scribbled all over it; what will become of you now?" Ch'en was in a great fright, and begged the young lady to intercede for him; to which she replied, "It was bad enough that you should come here and spy about; however, being a scholar, and a man of refinement, I would have done my best for you; but after this, how am I to help you?" Off she then ran with the handkerchief, while Ch'en remained behind in an agony of suspense, and longing for the wings of a bird to bear him away from his fate. By-and-by, the young lady returned and congratulated him, saying, "There is some hope for you. The Princess read your verses several times over, and was not at all angry. You will probably be released; but, meanwhile, wait here, and don't climb the trees, or try to get through the walls, or you may not escape after all."

Evening was now drawing on, and Ch'en knew not, for certain, what was about to happen; at the same time he was very empty, and, what with hunger and anxiety, death would have been almost a happy release. Before long, the young lady returned with a lamp in her hand, and followed by a slave-girl bearing wine and food, which she presented to Ch'en. He asked if there was any news about himself; to which the young lady replied that she had just mentioned his case to the Princess who, not knowing what to do with him at that hour of the night, had given orders that he should at once be provided with food, "which, at any rate," added she, "is not bad news."

The whole night long Ch'en walked up and down unable to take rest; and it was not till late in the morning that the young lady appeared with more food for him. Imploring her once more to intercede on his behalf, she told him that the Princess had not instructed them either to kill or to release him, and that it would not be fitting for such as herself to be bothering the Princess with suggestions. So there Ch'en still remained until another day had almost gone, hoping for the welcome moment; and then the young lady rushed hurriedly in, saying, "You are lost! Some one has told the Queen, and she, in a fit of anger, threw the handkerchief on the ground, and made use of very violent language. Oh dear! oh dear! I'm sure something dreadful will happen."

Ch'en threw himself on his knees, his face as pale as ashes, and begged to know what he should do } but at that moment sounds were heard outside, and the young lady waved her hand to him, and ran away. Immediately a crowd came pouring in through the door, with ropes ready to secure the object of their search ; and among them was a slave-girl, who looked fixedly at our hero, and cried out, "Why, surely you are Mr. Ch'en, aren't you ?" at the same time stopping the others from binding him until she should have reported to the Queen. In a few minutes she came back, and said the Queen requested him to walk in ; and in he went, through a number of doors, trembling all the time with fear, until he reached a hall, the screen before which was ornamented with green jade and silver.

A beautiful girl drew aside the bamboo curtain at the door, and announced, "Mr. Ch'en;" and he himself advanced, and fell down before a lady, who was sitting upon a dais at the other end, knocking his head upon the ground, and crying out, "Thy servant is from a far-off country; spare, oh! spare his life." "Sir! " replied the Queen, rising hastily from her seat, and extending a hand to Ch'en, "but for you, I should not be here today. Pray excuse the rudeness of my maids." Thereupon a splendid meal was served, and wine was poured out in chased goblets, to no small astonishment of Ch'en, who could not understand why he was treated thus. "Your kindness," observed the Queen, "in restoring me to life, I am quite unable to repay; however, as you have made my daughter the subject of your verse, the match is clearly ordained by fate, and I shall send her along to be your handmaid." Ch'en hardly knew what to make of this extraordinary accomplishment of his wishes, but the marriage was solemnized there and then; bands of music struck up wedding-airs, beautiful mats were laid down for them to walk upon, and the whole place was brilliantly lighted with a profusion of coloured lamps. Then Ch'en said to the Princess, "That a stray and unknown traveller like myself, guilty of spoiling your Highness's handkerchief, should have escaped the fate he deserved, was already more than could be expected; but now to receive you in marriage this, indeed, far surpasses my wildest expectations."

"My mother," replied the Princess, "is married to the King of this lake, and is herself a daughter of the River Prince. Last year, when on her way to visit her parents, she happened to cross the lake, and was wounded by an arrow; but you saved her life, and gave her plaster for the wound. Our family, therefore, is grateful to you, and can never forget your good act. And do not regard me as of another species than yourself; the Dragon King has bestowed upon me the elixir of immortality, and this I will gladly share with you." Then Ch'en knew that his wife was a spirit, and by-and-by he asked her how the slave-girl had recognised him; to which she replied, that the girl was the small fish which had been found hanging to the dolphin's tail. He then inquired why, as they didn't intend to kill him, he had been kept so long a prisoner. "I was charmed with your literary talent," answered the Princess, "but I did not venture to take the responsibility upon myself; and no one saw how I tossed and turned the livelong night."

"Dear friend," said Ch'en; "but, come, tell me who was it that brought my food." "A trusty waiting-maid of mine," replied the Princess; "her name is A-nien." Ch'en then asked how he could ever repay her, and the Princess told him there would be plenty of time to think of that; and when he inquired where the king, her father, was, she said he had gone off with the God of War to fight against Ch'ih-yu, and had not returned. A few days passed, and Ch'en began to think his people at home would be anxious about him; so he sent off his servant with a letter to tell them he was safe and sound, at which they were all overjoyed, believing him to have been lost in the wreck of the boat, of which event news had already reached them. However, they were unable to send him any reply, and were considerably distressed as to how he would find his way home again. Six months afterwards Ch'en himself appeared, dressed in fine clothes, and riding on a splendid horse, with plenty of money, and valuable jewels in his pocket evidently a man of wealth. From that time forth he kept up a magnificent establishment; and in seven or eight years had become the father of five children. Every day he kept open house, and if any one asked him about his adventures, he would readily tell them without reservation.

Now a friend of his, named Liang, whom he had known since they were boys together, and who, after holding an appointment for some years in Nan-fu, was crossing the Tung-t'ing Lake, on his way home, suddenly beheld an ornamental barge, with carved wood-work and red windows, passing over the foamy waves to the sound of music and singing from within. Just then a beautiful young lady leant out of one of the windows, which she had pushed open, and by her side Liang saw a young man sitting, while two nice-looking girls stood by and shampooed him. Liang, at first, thought it must be the party of some high official, and wondered at the scarcity of attendants; but, on looking more closely at the young man, he saw it was no other than his old friend Ch'en. Thereupon he began almost involuntarily to shout to him; and when Ch'en heard his own name, he stopped the rowers, and walked out beckoning Liang to cross over into his where the remains of their feast was quickly cle away, and fresh supplies of wine, and tea, and all kin of costly foods spread out by handsome slave-girls.

"It's ten years since we met," said Liang, "and what a rich man you have become in the meantime." "Well," replied Ch'en, "do you think that so very extraordinary for a poor fellow like me?" Liang then asked him who was the lady with whom he was taking wine, and Ch'en said she was his wife, which very much astonished Liang, who further inquired where they were going. "Westwards," answered Ch'en, and prevented any further questions by giving a signal for the music, which effectually put a stop to all further conversation. By-and-by, Liang found the wine getting into his head, and seized the opportunity to ask Ch'en to make him a present of one of his beautiful girls. "You are drunk, my friend," replied Ch'en; "however, I will give you the price of one as a pledge of our old friendship." And, turning to a servant, he bade him present Liang with a splendid pearl, saying, "Now you can buy a Green Pearl; you see I am not stingy;" adding forthwith, "but I am pressed for time, and can stay no longer with my old friend." So he escorted Liang back to his boat, and, having let go the rope, proceeded on his way. Now, when Liang reached home, and called at Ch'en's house, whom should he see but Ch'en himself drinking with a party of friends.

"Why, I saw you only yesterday," crien Liang, "upon the Tung-t'ing. How quickly you have got back!" Ch'en denied this, and then Liang repeated the whole story, at the conclusion of which, Ch'en laughed, and said, "You must be mistaken. Do you imagine I can be in two places at once?" The company were all much astonished, and knew not what to make of it; and subsequently when Ch'en, who died at the age of eighty, was being carried to his grave, the bearers thought the coffin seemed remarkably light, and on opening it to see, found that the body had disappeared.

SLAVIC REGION

THE STORY OF TREMSIN,
THE BIRD ZHAR AND NASTASIA,
THE LOVELY MAID OF THE SEA

ROBERT NISBET BAIN

ILLUSTRATIONS IVAN BILIBIN, BORIS ZVORKIN, E. W. MITCHELL

There was once upon a time a man and a woman, and they had one little boy. In the summertime they used to go out and mow corn in the fields, and one summer when they had laid their little lad by the side of a sheaf, an eagle swooped down, caught up the child, carried him into a forest, and laid him in its nest. Now in this forest three bandits chanced to be wandering at the same time. They heard the child crying in the eagle's nest: "Oo-oo! oo-oo! oo-oo!" so they went up to the oak on which was the nest and said one to another, "Let us hew down the tree and kill the child!" — "No," replied one of them, "it were better to climb up the tree and bring him down alive."

So he climbed up the tree and brought down the lad, and they nurtured him and gave him the name of Tremsin. They brought up Tremsin until he became a youth, and then they gave him a horse, set him upon it, and said to him, "Now go out into the wide world and search for thy father and thy mother!" So Tremsin went out into the wide world and pastured his steed on the vast steppes, and his steed spoke to him and said, "When we have gone a little farther, thou wilt see before thee a plume of the Bird Zhar; pick it not up, or sore trouble will be thine!" Then they went on again. They went on and on, through ten tsardoms they went, till they came to another empire in the land of Thrice Ten where lay the feather. And the youth said to himself, "Why should I not pick up the feather when it shines so brightly even from afar?"

And he went near to the feather, and it shone so that the like of it cannot be expressed or conceived or imagined or even told of in tales. Then Tremsin picked up the feather and went into the town over against him, and in that town there lived a rich nobleman. And Tremsin entered the house of this nobleman and said,

"Sir, may I not take service with thee as a labourer?" —
The nobleman looked at him, and seeing that he was
comely and stalwart, "Why not? Of course thou mayst,"
said he. So he took him into his service. Now this
nobleman had many servants, and they curried his
horses for him, and made them smart and glossy
against the day he should go hunting. And Tremsin
began to curry his horse likewise, and the servants of
the nobleman could not make the horses of their
master so shining bright as Tremsin made his own
horse. So they looked more closely, and they perceived
that when Tremsin cleaned his horse he stroked it
with the feather of the Bird Zhar, and the coat of the
good steed straightway shone like burnished silver.
Then those servants were filled with envy, and said
among themselves, "How can we remove this fellow
from the world? We'll saddle him with a task he is
unable to do, and then our master will drive him
away." —So they went to their master and said,
"Tremsin has a feather of the Bird Zhar, and he says
that if he likes he can get the Bird Zhar itself."

Then the nobleman sent for Tremsin and said to him,
"O Tremsin! my henchmen say that thou canst get the
Bird Zhar if thou dost choose." — "Nay, but I cannot,"
replied Tremsin. — "Answer me not," said the
nobleman, "for so sure as I've a sword, I'll slice thy
head off like a gourd." — Then Tremsin fell a-weeping
and went away to his horse. "My master," said he "hath

given me a task to do that will clean undo me."—"What task is that?" asked the horse. — "Why, to fetch him the Bird Zhar."—"Why that's not a task, but a trifle," replied the horse. "Let us go to the steppes," it continued, "and let me go a-browsing; but do thou strip thyself stark-naked and lie down in the grass, and the Bird Zhar will straightway swoop down to feed. So long as she only claws about thy body, touch her not; but as soon as she begins to claw at thine eyes, seize her by the legs."

So when they got to the wild steppes, Tremsin stripped himself naked and flung himself in the grass, and, immediately, the Bird Zhar swooped down and began pecking all about him, and at last she pecked at his eyes. Then Tremsin seized her by both legs, and mounted his horse and took the Bird Zhar to the nobleman. Then his fellow-servants were more envious than ever, and they said among themselves, "How shall we devise for him a task to do that cannot be done, and so rid the world of him altogether?" So they bethought them, and then they went to the nobleman and said, "Tremsin says that to get the Bird Zhar was nothing, and that he is also able to get the thrice-lovely Nastasia of the sea." Then the nobleman again sent for Tremsin and said to him, "Look now! thou didst get for me the Bird Zhar, see that thou now also gettest for me the thrice-lovely Nastasia of the sea." — "But I cannot, sir!" said Tremsin. — "Answer me not so!" replied the nobleman, "for so sure as I've a sword, I'll slice thy head off like a gourd an thou bring her not." —Then Tremsin went out to his horse and fell a-weeping. — "Wherefore dost thou weep?" asked the faithful steed.— "Wherefore should I not weep?" he replied. "My master has given me a task that cannot be done." — "What task is that?" — "Why, to fetch him the thrice-lovely Nastasia of the sea!" — "Oh-ho!" laughed the horse, "that is not a task, but a trifle. Go to thy master and say, 'Cause white tents to be raised by the sea-shore, and buy wares of sundry kinds, and wine and spirits in bottles and flasks,' and the thrice-lovely Nastasia will come and purchase thy wares, and then thou mayst take her."

"Since thou hast found the feather of the Bird Zhar, and the Bird Zhar herself."

And the nobleman did so. He caused white tents to be pitched by the sea-shore, and bought kerchiefs and scarves and spread them out gaily, and made great store of wine and brandy in bottles and flasks. Then Tremsin rode toward the tents, and while he was on the way his horse said to him, "Now when I go to graze, do thou lie down and feign to sleep. Then the thrice-lovely Nastasia will appear and say, 'What for thy wares?' but do thou keep silence. But when she begins to taste of the wine and the brandy, then she will go to sleep in the tent, and thou canst catch her easily and hold her fast!" Then Tremsin lay down and feigned to sleep, and forth from the sea came the thrice-lovely Nastasia, and went up to the tents and asked, "Merchant, merchant, what for thy wares?" But he lay there, and moved never a limb. She asked the same thing over and over again, but, getting no answer, went into the tents where stood the flasks and the bottles. She tasted of the wine. How good it was! She tasted of the brandy. That was still better. So from tasting she fell to drinking. First she drank a little, and then she drank a little more, and at last she went asleep in the tent. Then Tremsin seized the thrice-lovely Nastasia and put her behind him on horseback, and carried her off to the nobleman. The nobleman praised Tremsin exceedingly, but the thrice-lovely Nastasia said, "Look now! since thou hast found the feather of the Bird Zhar, and the Bird Zhar herself, since also thou hast found me, thou must now fetch me also my little coral necklace from the sea!"

Then Tremsin went out to his faithful steed and wept sorely, and told him all about it. And the horse said to him, "Did I not tell thee that grievous woe would come upon thee if thou didst pick up that feather?" But the horse added, "Come! weep not! after all 'tis not a task, but a trifle." Then they went along by the sea, and the horse said to him, "Let me out to graze, and then keep watch till thou seest a crab come forth from the sea, and then say to him, 'I'll catch thee.'" —So Tremsin let his horse out to graze, and he himself stood by the sea-shore, and watched and watched till he saw a crab come swimming along. Then he said to the crab, "I'll catch thee." — "Oh! seize me not!" said the crab, "but let me get back into the sea, and I'll be of great service to thee." — "Very well," said Tremsin, "but thou must get me from the sea the coral necklace of the thrice-lovely Nastasia," and with that he let the crab go back into the sea again. Then the crab called together all her young crabs, and they collected all the coral and brought it ashore, and gave it to Tremsin. Then the faithful steed came running up, and Tremsin mounted it, and took the coral to the thrice-lovely Nastasia.

"Well," said Nastasia, "thou hast got the feather of the Bird Zhar, thou hast got the Bird Zhar itself, thou hast got me my coral, get me now from the sea my herd of wild horses!" Then Tremsin was sore distressed, and went to his faithful steed and wept bitterly, and told him all about it. "Well," said the horse, "this time 'tis no trifle, but a real hard task. Go now to thy master, and bid him buy twenty hides, and twenty poods of pitch, and twenty poods of flax, and twenty poods of hair." — So Tremsin went to his master and told him, and his master bought it all. Then Tremsin loaded his horse with all this, and to the sea they went together. And when they came to the sea the horse said, "Now lay upon me the hides and the tar and the flax, and lay them in this order—first a hide, and then a pood of tar, and then a pood of flax, and so on, laying them thus till they are all laid." Tremsin did so.

"And now," said the horse, "I shall plunge into the sea, and when thou seest a large red wave driving toward the shore, run away till the red wave has passed and thou dost see a white wave coming, and then sit down on the shore and keep watch. I shall then come out of the sea, and after me the whole herd; then thou must strike with the horsehair the horse which gallops immediately after me, and he will not be too strong for thee." —So the faithful steed plunged into the sea, and Tremsin sat down on the shore and watched. The horse swam to a bosquet that rose out of the sea, and there the herd of sea-horses was grazing. When the strong charger of Nastasia saw him and the hides he carried on his back, it set off after him at full tilt, and the whole herd followed the strong charger of

Nastasia. They drove the horse with the hides into the sea, and pursued him. Then the strong charger of Nastasia caught up the steed of Tremsin and tore off one of his hides, and began to worry it with his teeth and tear it to fragments as he ran. Then he caught him up a second time, and tore off another hide, and began to worry that in like manner till he had torn it also to shreds; and thus he ran after Tremsin's steed for seventy miles, till he had torn off all the hides, and worried them to bits.

But Tremsin sat upon the sea-shore till he saw the large white billow bounding in, and behind the billow came his own horse, and behind his own horse came the thrice-terrible charger of the thrice-lovely Nastasia, with the whole herd at his heels.

"They drove the horse with the hides into the sea, and pursued him."

Tremsin struck him full on the forehead with the twenty poods of hair, and immediately he stood stock still. Then Tremsin threw a halter over him, mounted, and drove the whole herd to the thrice-lovely Nastasia. Nastasia praised Tremsin for his prowess, and said to him, "Well, thou hast got the feather of the Bird Zhar, thou hast got the Bird Zhar itself, thou hast got me my coral and my herd of horses, now milk my mare and put the milk into three vats, so that there may be milk hot as boiling water in the first vat, lukewarm milk in the second vat, and icy cold milk in the third vat." Then Tremsin went to his faithful steed and wept bitterly, and the horse said to him, "Wherefore dost thou weep?" — "Why should I not weep?" cried he; "the thrice-lovely Nastasia has given me a task to do that cannot be done. I am to fill three vats with the milk from her mare, and the milk must be boiling hot in the first vat, and lukewarm in the second, and icy cold in the third vat." — "Oh-ho!" cried the horse, "that is not a task, but a trifle. I'll caress the mare, and then go on nibbling till thou hast milked all three vats full." So Tremsin did so. He milked the three vats full, and the milk in the first vat was boiling hot, and in the second vat warm, and in the third vat freezing cold.

When all was ready the thrice-lovely Nastasia said to Tremsin, "Now, leap first of all into the cold vat, and then into the warm vat, and then into the boiling hot vat!" —Tremsin leaped into the first vat, and leaped out again an old man; he leaped into the second vat, and leaped out again a youth; he leaped into the third vat, but when he leaped out again, he was so young and handsome that no pen can describe it, and no tale can tell of it. Then the thrice-lovely Nastasia herself leaped into the vats. She leaped into the first vat, and came out an old woman; she leaped into the second vat, and came out a young maid; but when she leaped out of the third vat, she was so handsome and goodly that no pen can describe it, and no tale can tell of it. Then the thrice-lovely Nastasia made the nobleman leap into the vats. He leaped into the first vat, and became quite old; he leaped into the second vat, and became quite young; he leaped into the third vat, and burst to pieces. Then Tremsin took unto himself the thrice-lovely Nastasia to wife, and they lived happily together on the nobleman's estate, and the evil servants they drove right away.

THE END

What to do next?
You can read many more fairy tales on

fairytalez.com

Printed in Poland
by Amazon Fulfillment
Poland Sp. z o.o., Wrocław